The Lost and Found

Book One

By

S.S. Magrogan

Bloomington, IN

Milton Keynes, UK

AuthorHouse™
1663 Liberty Drive, Suite 200
Bloomington, IN 47403
www.authorhouse.com
Phone: 1-800-839-8640

AuthorHouse™ UK Ltd.
500 Avebury Boulevard
Central Milton Keynes, MK9 2BE
www.authorhouse.co.uk
Phone: 08001974150

First published by AuthorHouse 4/14/2006

ISBN: 1-4259-2339-9 (sc)
ISBN: 1-4259-2340-2 (dj)

Library of Congress Control Number: 2006902336

Printed in the United States of America
Bloomington, Indiana

This book is printed on acid-free paper.

The Lost and Found

To my twinkie, Jaz, who believed in the existence of frits and that I wasn't crazy for wanting to write a book about them.

1

Banished

This is a tale of epic proportions, starting long ago and happening even now; but if I tell it to you, you'll probably forget, for *that* is the way of a frit.

"A frit", you say, "I've never seen or heard about one of those."

Well, actually you have. You just forgot. That is what I am trying to tell you, just like the wise old frit leader tried to tell some of the youth in his tribe, many years ago.

It was high noon, and the sun was bearing down on the meadow beside a neighborhood playground. And there in the center of the meadow was a large oak tree with a hole in the bottom of its trunk. Inside the cool shade of the tree trunk stood a small creature no bigger than your hand. He looked just like a small magical creature should look, almost human, but not quite, with small black beady eyes and a face strewn with what looked like swirling lines of ink on his cheeks and forehead. His long gray beard was braided into seven separate braids and his hair was made of what could only be described as, and was, quite literally, dust.

Showing in his kind and counseling demeanor, was the wisdom he had acquired through the years, which he offered freely to his kind to help them through the trials of living with man; and on this day, he had offered to teach the young about their history.

So, as a light autumn breeze blew through the tree trunk, the wise old frit leader used his chubby four- fingered hand to tuck his hair of grey flowing dust behind his ear so he could see the little ones before him. He so loved teaching the young; they were so full of life and hope.

Smiling as he smoothed out the wrinkles on his tan linen robe and fastened the key on his big leather belt a little tighter, he sat down on the floor of the tree trunk facing three smaller creatures all with flowing hair of dust and beady black eyes reflecting an eagerness to listen and to learn. He wondered if they would like a repeat lesson, the most important lesson of all. The littlest one looked up at him with eager eyes, seeming to know the elder's thoughts

"Will you tell the story again, Elder ElCa.?"

"Sure, my little one.", said ElCa surveying his pupils to make sure that each one was paying attention.

"Thousands of years ago, we, the frits, could be found on the Earth as keepers of the Magic Forest. Because we were keepers of the magical realm, we had magic power to make mankind forget the entrance to the forest, so that all magic creatures could be protected. We were responsible with our magic and over time we used it to influence and help mankind in their daily endeavors. We helped many a forlorn lover forget the memories of the love they lost. We helped many a shaken leader of a good cause to remember their courage and forget their hate. We even helped a miser or two, forget their material possessions so that they could use their wealth to help others. Through it all, we were never seen. And if we were seen, we made mankind forget that as well. Do you have the spell memorized yet, my little ones?"

The three small frits nodded eagerly awaiting the chance to prove their knowledge. The elder saw their willingness to recite and promptly asked them to do so.

"RECITE!"

The little frits stood up from the ground of the Great Oak. Each placed a different sock with two holes cut out in the front, over their entire bodies, took out a small feather and held it out from under their sock. They spoke in semi-unison saying, "May your forgetfulness be dust upon the heads of all frits present. Forget that you have seen this sock. May your forgetfulness be dust upon the heads of all frits present."

The small frits each whisked the air from their mouths with their bird feathers towards the opening of the trunk and towards children playing on a nearby playground. They waited for but a small moment for proof positive that their spell had worked. Two of the little ones squealed in delight as the dusty hair on their heads began to grow just enough to cover their eyes.

"It worked." one screamed from underneath a red and green argyle sock.

"Me too." the other one yelled as he took off the pink and white duck sock and flicked his dusty bangs to show how long they had grown. The tallest of the three, wearing a brown sock with a hole in the heel was still turning in circles whisking the air from the trunk out of the opening with his feather. ElCa quickly stopped the dizzying frit from spinning, helped him get his sock off, and sat him gently back down on the dirt floor. The other two frits followed and knelt before the elder.

"That was fritatstic my little dust bunnies. Now, why do we make humans forget they have seen a sock rather than just forget that they have seen a frit?" The chubbiest of the little ones raised his hand.

"Yes Onda, do you want to answer this question?" Onda nodded, stood up and cleared his throat in preparation for answering the elder.

"It is easier to make a human forget that they have seen a sock than to make them forget they have seen a frit."

"Well done Onda. Now do you want me to continue with the history of our kind?"

The tiny frits all nodded "yes" and leaned in closer to the elder to hear his words.

"For thousands of years, our ancestors made beautiful homes in the forest and even helped other magical creatures to come and live in the magic realm. Do you know what it is called when you have the right to live in the Magic Forest?"

The smallest of the little frits raised his hand and hopped up and down on his knees to get the elder's attention.

"Yes, Amry, would you like to answer?" Amry stood up and spoke loudly for all to hear.

"When a magical creature wants to reside in the Magic Forest for protection from mankind or to retire from working in the human world, they must obtain the privilege of Ancient Magical Creature Status other wise called AMCS."

"Well done, Amry. Now, do any of you have questions about AMCS?"

Onda raised his hand again, "Can any creature get status, elder?"

"Oh no, Onda, only truly magical creatures that have existed for a thousand or more years and wish to reside in the Magic Forest can have this status. If it weren't so, birds, mice, and toads would have AMCS, as they commonly wander into the forest, but they don't possess magic.

"Elder, how come we don't have status anymore? We're ancient, we're magical, and we want to live in the forest again?" Amry spoke out of turn which made the elder frown, but he answered the question anyway.

"Oh my little one, this is the hard part of the story to tell. Now, our kind lived in the Magic Forest for nearly 6000 years. Our AMCS was never threatened or denied, that is until Oletta came." Elca looked up to the light streaming in from the upper part of the trunk and casting interesting shadows on the wall. He knew that he must be careful not to excite the little ones and bring them to hate their fellow magic creatures. He closed his eyes and gathered strength from within to assemble words which would help the young frits understand history but not repeat it. He opened his eyes when he felt the tallest frit tugging on the key that was attached to the belt of his robe.

"Yes, Yo?"

"ElCa, I think my feather is broken, my hair didn't grow like Amry's or Onda's. Do I still get to be a frit?" Yo stood staring at the leader, mouth open and eyes as wide as a forlorn puppy dog.

"Dear little fritter, don't worry. You'll get the spell down soon enough. And when class is over, I will help you pick out a new feather. Now sit back down."

Elca decided that he had the words to express the plight of their kind and to help the little ones understand that all hope wasn't lost, so he continued on with his lesson.

"You see, little ones, Queen Oletta wasn't always a queen. She entered the forest with her mother, THE fairy godmother. All the fairies came from far and wide seeking AMCS so that they could live under the protection of the magic realm. You see, the fairies had been living with humans for quite some time and were being captured or worse, seen, more often than not; and they desperately needed to get away. So, the AMCS council granted them that status. The fairies, our ancestors, and many different kinds of magical creatures lived in harmony for quite some time until something happened in the human world that we could not prevent."

Yo stood up and raised his hand higher and higher to get the old leader's attention.

"Yes Yo, do you have something else to add to the class?"

Yo kept his arm up while he answered the leader,

"Is this when raisins were invented?"

Amry and Onda snickered and ElCa quickly shushed them and sat Yo back down on the dirt floor.

"No, Yo, now pay attention." Yo hung his head, he was sure that he would have got that one right. ElCa straightened his robe and continued with his lecture.

"Around the early 1800's, in mankind years, stories were being collected about humans that had actually seen magical creatures. The Magic Forest was in a great upheaval. Magic creatures were NOT to be seen. What creature could have violated this rule? Everyone was asking. Everyone was being questioned. It was soon enough when it was revealed that Oletta, the fairy godmother's daughter, had traveled to the human world and had shown herself to the authors of these stories and had promised to show them more if they wrote more stories about fairies. The authors agreed to write a book called "Fairy Tales" as long as Oletta revealed more of the magic realm to them."

Elca looked down at the little frits and saw that they were in shock and in awe. He moved the story along.

"With a heavy heart, AMCS council decided to hold a special meeting. All the magical creatures' leaders were there, Elder Zebedee of the frits, King Ellinvaughn I of the elves, King Gollywink of the dwarves, Master Dragon Ragule, and even the Fairy Godmother. They deliberated and discussed whether or not the AMCS status of the fairies should be revoked since one of their kind had broken the most important rule of all of never being seen, on purpose that is. Fairy Godmother was upset but she knew that this must be the way. She understood that her daughter's actions had consequences.

The council was about to make a decision on the matter when Oletta, burst through the door of the council meeting and who should be with her but one of the human authors of Fairy Tales. All three little frits gasped in horror at the fact of a magic creature bringing a human to the Magic Forest.

"What happened next ElCa?" Amry stood up from the dirt floor and began to pace. He was unusually nervous and wound up for a little frit.

"Come here, Amry and sit in my lap. I will finish the story." ElCa pulled Amry down onto his lap and wrapped his arms around him in a hug and whispered, "It's going to be alright Amry. Calm down." Amry's breathing slowed and he stopped biting his fingernails.

"Okay, now what happened next was a shock to all frit kind. Oletta asked permission to address the council. Of course they all wanted to hear her reasons for bringing a human into the forest; so, they let her speak. She said that the human she had with her was one of the Brothers Grimm. He and his brother had been collecting rare stories about how humans came to realize that magical creatures were impacting their lives. These were remarkable stories indeed and would ensure magical creatures to be immortalized in the human world. However, she had reviewed all the stories containing dragons, trolls, elves, fairies, and to her surprise, there were no stories about frits. She told the council that frit-kind apparently did not exist to the humans because they spent their magic on making mankind forget; and therefore, they should not have the right to live in the magic realm. Our elder, Zebedee, stood up and told the council that her suggestion was outrageous. He told the council that frits make humans forget what they have seen or silly things that they don't need, for the betterment of mankind, and it's quite obvious that frits exist. Oletta interrupted and said that Zebedee was perpetuating a lie that the frits had any magic at all, maybe that's why there were no stories of them and if they could make people forget, who's to say that they wouldn't make all magic kind forget their own powers and then take over the forest."

"I don't believe it!" said Amry as he jumped out of ElCa's lap and clenched his fists preparing to punch into the air.

"She's the one that broke the rule. She should have been thrown out!" yelled Onda as he looked to Amry for approval of his assessment of the situation.

"I always thought that fairies were supposed to be pretty and smell like strawberries." said Yo as he drew a picture of a strawberry on the dirt floor of the tree trunk with a stick.

"If you let me continue, I will tell you the rest." ElCa shushed his pupils and motioned for them to take their seats back on the dirt floor and took the stick from Yo to stop him from doodling.

"After Oletta and Zebedee finished an unusually long shouting match, there was much talking and grumbling in the council chambers and it wasn't long before the council decided to take a vote. And vote they did; right then and there to revoke the frits' AMCS status and to make Oletta the queen of the Magic Forest since she had done so much to keep the memory of all magical creatures alive in the human world and all the frits had done, supposedly, was make mankind forget. It was a sad day my little ones, a sad day. Our forefathers were banished from the forest and we have lived with mankind ever since."

Amry began to cry, Onda cleared his throat and Yo drew more pictures on the dirt with his chubby little finger. ElCa and the little ones were upset and they should've been, because the rest of the story does not get any better. When their kind was banished from the Magic Forest, and entered the human world, they lost their ability to be immortal and the women began having terrible pains with their childbirth, much like mankind. They all knew it wouldn't be easy living among the humans and the new fairy queen didn't make it any easier for them either. She was so irate with being yelled at by Zebedee that she decided to put a curse on them to make sure that bearing new baby frits in the world would be almost impossible.

Legend has it that Queen Oletta had just been given a newly forged scepter as a token of loyalty, by the elves, who feared that their number was up if they didn't appease the young queen. This scepter of power would only work if the owner had been given a special elvish password and if he or she said it correctly over the scepter. Oletta was given such a word and she spoke perfect elvish. Once the scepter was turned on, if you will, it gave the owner the power to speak a blessing or a curse and have it exacted upon the creature for which the curse or blessing was being said. The elves had hoped that Queen Oletta would use it to bless magic kind in their new era of being discovered by the humans. However, she decided to use it to endanger frit-kind forever.

She held it high above the frit throng as they gathered their belongings and prepared to leave the Magic Forest. She hovered high in the clouds and spoke these words, "I smite you with a terrible curse. You must be moved by man at the time of your birth. If they do not move you, you will not be born. The curse begins at the blowing of my French horn." The queen pulled out a beautiful brass horn and blew on it hard, almost in a way to say to the frits that it was their time to go, depart, and die.

Queen Oletta knew that all frits obeyed the rule of never being seen by man, so to place on them this curse would have them violate their own rule. If they did not abide by the curse, they would never be able to bear children. She thought that surely, this curse would keep the frits from having babies; and then they would dwindle down to nothing. She was wrong.

As the frits exited the forest and began their term of banishment, there were many fritlies (frit ladies) that were due for giving birth. Something had to be figured out right away. At first, the frit fathers tried to outsmart the curse and simply run and carry their wives but when they stopped; the frit mother would undergo terrible labor pains and still not be able to have the baby. The fathers then realized that they would *have* to use humans to satisfy the curse.

They learned to place the expecting mothers into the saddle bags of a horse rider's horse. The father would make the owner of the horse forget where he was going and he would ride around for hours before he would remember. Eventually the rider would stop due to confusion and the mother, who at this point had plenty of time to have the baby, would escape down the reigns of the horse onto the ground. Although, it has been said that the fritlies did not find this manner of birthing appealing, since it made them smell like horse rear end for a week or two.

Many years later, frit mothers and their babies had a little more comfortable and less smelly way to give birth and to be moved by man all at the same time by hopping into the doors of mankind's latest invention, the carriage. It would seem that Queen Oletta's curse was not working as she had planned; and by the early 1900's, frits were being born everywhere due to the invention of the automobile.

Cars were everywhere and easy to get into by the frits, which aided the fritmunity to grow by leaps and bounds; and the queen was left to wonder where she went wrong with her curse. She wondered for many years how she could destroy the frits once and for all. And for many years she worked on devising an evil plan to do just that. Unfortunately, for the frit, her evil designs were spelled out quite clearly at the Great Oak Gathering of 1937.

The queen had sent word by the ravens that inhabited the Magic Forest to ask for all the frit-kind to return to the entrance of the forest, the very oak tree that I mentioned before. She sent the birds because all magic folk speak "bird"; and she was unwilling to do such tedious work herself. The birds told as many frits as they could, that Queen Oletta had realized that they had suffered enough and that she felt bad about her curse and was willing to let them all back in. The frits took the ravens' message to heart and decided to gather under the Great Oak, just as the queen had requested, with great hope and anticipation in being let back into their rightful dwelling place. They waited for what seemed a long time for the queen to arrive.

She appeared, with great fanfare and once again, placed her scepter of power high in the air. All frits gasped at the thought of finally being let back into the home of their fathers, but ironic as it seemed, they *forgot* how evil and conniving their queen was. She spoke an addendum to the curse hoping to be rid of them for all time.

These were her very words, "You will forever be born in cars, this is true. And I have a final promise for you. If the car you are born in, moves again, in its original way, you will die the very same day."

The frits were stunned and they stared at the queen as she fluttered her glittery wings and disappeared through the Great Oak.

"How could she?", some asked.

"Why would she?", some cried.

Some frits began disappearing from the crowd almost immediately, turning into strands of dust as the cars they had been born in were moving, going to the grocery store or to the movies.

As the questions flew and frits everywhere were dying, they realized that many frits had forgotten what car they were born in and thus were doomed to die unless they remembered and made the owner forget how to drive or where he put his keys. They knew they had to come up with a way, fast, to remember what car they had been born in and how to keep the cars from moving again, once their babies were born.

The leader of the frits at that time, Zeqoyia, was thinking hard on devising a plan that all frits could easily use to save themselves and their newborns. But, sad to say, as he was finding a way for the frits to live, there were other frits who were anxiously engaged in thinking up a way for Queen Oletta to die, or at least steal her scepter of power. It is a divide that exists among the fritmunity even now. Zeqoyia had a difficult time gathering all the frits that were left to tell them of his life saving plan for many were too focused on the plan of revenge against the queen.

He did what he could to gather all those who would listen back at the base of the Great Oak and told them the plan. Its quite simple really, I could go on, however, I know of someone who is giving a news report on that very plan right now, that little frit who sat on Elca's lap, years ago, learning the history of his kind. He is a reporter for the Fritscovery news channel now; and he can bring you up to speed. (Yes, I know, it's a frit joke, but you'll forget it, don't worry.)

2

Fritscovery News at 7:59

Amry was not in the mood that afternoon to do a report that he found silly and mundane. *I don't know why Ocus wants me to do a story on a frit birth in the first place. Everyone already knows how it happens and why we do the things we do, its, well…* Amry realized that he was thinking out loud and quickly quieted his thoughts as he put on his pink and yellow duck sock and headed down the sidewalk of a quiet neighborhood. He kept his feather out just in case he needed to say the forgetting spell.

The afternoon sun shone on the houses of Ginkgo Street, which was located in a neighborhood where all of the streets were named after the many trees that grew along the sidewalks there. As Amry shuffled down the shadowed sidewalk, he played a game with himself in seeing how many of the street or rather tree names that he had memorized. *Let's see now, there's Hickory, Maple, Pine, Magnolia, Oak, Willow and…oh for dust's sake, what is that last one?* Amry hopped up into the air with surprise when a voice from behind him said, "Cypress!"

"Dust it all, Onda, don't you know there could be humans around. Shut your lint trap!" Amry lifted up the bottom of his sock covering so that he could give his red and green argyle sock covered friend, the evil eye.

'What?! I already said the spell like eight hundred times, see? Look at my dust?" Amry's friend and camera man, Onda, pulled up his sock and flicked his dusty bangs to show how they were nearly covering his face.

"Where are we headed anyway?" Onda asked as he pulled his red and green sock back down over his body. Amry pushed his sock back down and seemed to mumble as he answered Onda.

"Ocus told me that the expecting parents are supposed to be just a few houses down this way. We are supposed to wait for them to catch a car and then begin the interview."

"What interview?", asked Onda who quickly realized that a car was slowly moving up the street towards them. Onda grabbed the back of Amry's sock and pushed him behind a tree trunk.

"Say the spell Onda." whispered Amry as he and Onda both took out their word feathers. But before Onda could open his mouth, he and Amry both saw a frit jump out of the bright yellow car when it came to a stop in front of a blue house with windows all in the front. This frit put on a black sock and began waving a feather towards the cab driver and the passenger.

"Is that our interview?" inquired Onda as he put his feather away.

"No, Onda, that's a taxicab. Haven't you ever seen one of those before?" Amry put his feather away in his satchel and pulled out a small felt covered lapel microphone that he had conveniently made a human forget about. He unwound the wire from around the mike and handed the end to Onda who was pulling a pen camera out of a sling that he wore around his chest.

"Plug this in, ya big dust bunny. We have got to get over there before the whole ceremony is over with." Amry shook the end of the microphone at Onda until he noticed it and plugged it into the side of the tiny pen camera that he had magically made its owner forget.

"Don't get your lint in a ball! I'm on it," he made sure that the camera was charged and that the lighting was reasonable. Amry and Onda put their socks back on and said the forgetting spell, just in case, waving their words towards the cabby who was helping the passenger from the car collect their packages and books and take them to the front door of the blue house. As they walked over to the bright yellow cab, Amry did a mike check.

"Check one, check, check, check, checkity, chackity, chuckity, cheekity, check." Amry chuckled on that last "check" because he knew that the whole mike check infuriated Onda. And Onda was all too quick to remind Amry of that very fact.

"If you check one more time, I am going to see that you get "checked" into a facility for the frits with dust for brains."

"Come on, let's catch up with the expecting father." Amry said as he gestured for Onda to pick up the pace and catch up with a frit who was terribly out of breath and standing right underneath the taxi.

Amry positioned himself right next to the frit father and straightened his black leather vest and buttons, stuck out his chest, and held up the microphone with his four knobby fingers. "In one, two, three," he said as Onda focused the camera on him.

"Amry here for the local CRUD at 7:59…." Amry drew a cheeky smile from his lips and stuck his tongue out at Onda.

"Stop it!" said Onda, almost dropping the camera to the ground as he covered his mouth for a slight giggle. "You better stop doing that. I might forget to edit it out next time."

Amry pointed his fingers and moved it in small circles in front of Onda's face chanting in a low voice, "For-g-e-t, for-g-e-t." Amry chuckled from his joke.

"That's not how the forgetting charm works; you know that. Now do the report right," said Onda as he picked up his camera, "In one, two, and three…."

Amry showed another cheeky grin on his face and muttered, "Well, it worked on your mom."

"Cut-it-out Amry," Onda frowned and pointed to the center of the camera lens, "In one, two three…."

"Amry here, for the local report at 7:59. Tonight the Fritscovery Channel News brings you up close to a frit birth. We all know that it is not easy ducking the fairy queen's terrible curse while starting your new family. It's even harder to give an interview during the whole process; but tonight, we have found a couple that seems to have it all together: Chev and Coop."

Amry directed Onda to point the camera at the unusually long haired frit standing next to him while he began the line of questioning for the interview.

"So, Chev, tell the audience how it's done. How do we keep our new mothers and babies moving in a car during birth; and how do we stop the car from moving in its original way again, once the baby is born?"

"Yes…I umm…" Chev realized that his newly grown hair, from all the spell speaking he had done earlier, was getting in the way of his ability to speak or even see the camera. Amry waved to Onda to film the taxicab while he helped Chev out. "Here is a rubber band. Just put your hair back like this and give Onda the thumb's up when you're ready to go."

Chev put his newly grown hair into a pony tail, took a deep breath, spread his hands out in front, as if to center himself, and gave Onda the thumb's up sign. Onda pointed the pen-cam at Chev and gave the thumbs up sign back to Amry. Chev started the interview again.

"Okay, well, we, Coop and I, live just a few blocks from here, right next to the library. And while Coop was cleaning up after breakfast, she started having terrible labor pains, so I knew that we had to find a car right away. The owner of the house, where we live, was already gone for the day to go to work, so we knew that we would have to walk down the street and find another car to have the baby. We walked just a few feet to the library parking lot, because it was our back up place to look for a car in case our first choice of car failed. We put on our socks, which was hard to do since Coop has gotten bigger these past few weeks; and I had to really tug to get that sock over her. I said the forgetting spell so that all the people walking in and out of the library wouldn't see us. I said it so many times that my hair grew fast; I could barely see where I was going." Chev flicked his pony tail at the camera.

Amry looked into the camera and said, "Wow! That's quite a hair growing story you got there. What happened next?" Amry put the lapel mike back in front of Chev so he could finish the interview.

"Okay, well, the first car that stopped in the library parking lot was this taxicab." Chev pointed to the undercarriage of the car parked over them. "The passenger was carrying a lot of books and as the cab driver got out of the cab to help the passenger with her books, my wife and I hopped in and slid under the driver's side seat. My wife is still there, so if you'll excuse me." Chev hopped through the driver's side door of the cab which he had earlier made the cab driver forget to shut.

Amry quickly tried to get one more question in, "Chev, do you think it's a boy or a girl?"

"No time to talk now, Amry. I have got to get my wife, my baby and the car keys out of this cab!" Chev pointed to the fact that the cab driver was coming down the driveway of the blue house and heading back to the driver's side door of the cab. Chev put on his sock and said the forgetting spell one more time, waving his feather towards the cab driver whose feet were walking right towards him. Amry and Onda were safe underneath the cab; but Amry wanted to venture out and get a better shot at what was going on.

"Onda point that camera up at the driver of the cab. We've got to let our audience see this!" Onda snuck the edge of the camera out from underneath the cab, focusing it on the movement of the cab driver's feet and also the feet of Chev and his family. Amry watched in amazement as the escape from the cab commenced.

"Did you see that?" Amry whispered into the microphone as he pointed to the cab for Onda to film the new father leaping into the cab when the door was open, barely missing the foot of the driver and leaping back out with his new baby and wife, all the while wearing his sock and waving his spell feather furiously and dragging a set of keys behind him.

"AMAZING! Dust in the wind folks, DUST-IN-THE-WIND!" whispered Amry has he helped pull Chev and his new family, back under the cab. Chev was seemingly out of breath; but he had just enough left to tell Amry what they must do next.

"I have taken the car keys out of the ignition and I must hide them now so that they will never be found. I never want that car to move again in its original way. Yes, I know the owner can have new keys made but that can't hurt my new baby, only these original ones can do damage. Can you help my wife and child across the street to stand behind that mail box? We have to get out of here because the cab driver will definitely look under the car for his keys."

Amry and Onda quickly detached the mike from the camera, rolled up the wire and put on their socks to escort Chev's wife, and their new baby across the street all the while saying the forgetting spell in case the cab driver was looking their way. Amry's hair grew down to his feet during the trip across the street and he nearly tripped over his newly grown dust trying to climb up the street curb and help Coop and her new baby hide behind the pole of a mail box.

"Onda, look inside my satchel and see if I have another rubber band in there. I can't see a thing." Onda took off his sock and lifted up Amry's sock as well. He rummaged through Amry's satchel until he found a small rubber band and placed it in Amry's hand.

"Well, that was definitely exhilarating." said Amry as he tied his hair up, took his sock off and shoved it back into his satchel, and unwound the mike wire to hand to Onda to plug back into the pen-cam. Onda wasn't paying attention to Amry though; he was helping Coop out of her sock which had gotten stuck over her and her new baby.

"Get over here and help me Amry. Worry about the interview later!" Onda yelled as he tugged really hard on Coop's black and red checkered sock. He nearly knocked her and her new child over with that last tug. Seeing the potential disaster unfolding before him, Amry stood right behind Coop to steady her from falling backwards.

Coop was not impressed with their efforts and was about to give both of them a complete dusting when she peered out from behind the mail box to see her husband in his black sock, running towards them. Onda and Amry saw it too.

"Plug the mike in, Onda, our story is returning." Amry threw the mike wire to Onda who plugged it in, turned the camera back on, and pointed it towards the street. Chev ran towards them; and when he was safely behind the mailbox, he took off his sock. He was out of breath again, but it didn't seem to bother him because he began jabbering into Amry's mike about what had just transpired across the street.

"DUST PAN! You should've seen it. I took the car keys out of the cab so that the taxi could no longer run in its original way- you know to satisfy the curse. And I made the cab driver forget that he had seen a sock. I also made the cab driver forget where he had placed his keys so he would start looking all around for them. I can't believe I did that while I was still standing under the cab. That driver kept looking under the car and on the ground and now look." Chev pointed to his pony tail which was now dragging the ground.

"I didn't know that I could say the forgetting spell, that many times in a minute. So, as you know Amry, for my new um….", Chev stopped and turned to look at his wife and new born to see if he had a boy or a girl. His wife lifted up the baby booty which was covering the baby to protect it from being seen. Chev jumped up and down and said, "My new baby girl. I have a girl, Amry! Oh, the interview. Sorry. So, as you know, for my new baby girl to live, I must never let the cab driver find these keys, for if he places these keys back into the cab's ignition, and drives that car again, in its original way, my new daughter will be dust to dust. So if you will excuse me, I have some hiding to do." Chev put his sock back on and ran around to the back of the house that was behind them. Amry and Onda kept filming the taxicab and its driver, who was now dialing on his cell phone.

Just as a tow truck pulled up to take the cab and its driver away, Chev returned. Hiding his daughter's birth-keys had obviously caused him to be too out of breath to continue with the interview so they all decided to wait for Chev to regain his composure by filming and watching the cab driver get into the tow truck, which was now hooked up to the taxicab, and pulling away. They all gave a sigh of relief and Amry asked Onda, once again, to point the camera at the new family. This time, Amry decided to let the mother do some of the talking seeing as the new father was just too tired at this point.

"Coop, would you tell our audience how we name our children and why we name them the way that we do, and then, if you're ready, you can announce the name of your new baby girl?" Amry trailed off as he waited for a reply from the new mother who looked at her husband for approval before speaking the name.

"Well, Amry, as all frit-kind knows, many of our ancestors were lost in the Great Oak gathering of 1937, because they forgot what car they had been born in and were unable to make the owner forget where they placed their keys. Today, thanks to the leader back in 1937, we have a special naming system to protect us from forgetting where we were born in case we need to get back to our birth car and hide the keys again, should the owner find them. It is true that birth keys usually resurface before their owner in about seven years and there is nothing we can do about that. Seven years is long enough for us to live in the human world. But we increase our chances of living or escaping the queen's curse by the way we name our children. We use a four- letter segment of the car make or model to name our children.

Why only four letters? Its said that we only use four letters to keep the fairy queen from coming up with another curse to kill all frits named after the same type of car and if we only use four letters of the car name, we will all have many different names and can survive. With that said, we have chosen the name ICAB for our daughter. And I just want to add that I am so proud of my husband today. He took and hid her birth-keys so well that I am sure our daughter will live a long and happy life."

"Coop, she will, she will," said Amry, smirking a little and narrowing his brow. He stared into the camera and added, "She may live long, but will she be happy in the nomadic existence forced upon us by Queen Oletta and the Ancient Magical Creature Society? I think not."

"Not again," muttered Onda gloomily. Chev and Coop gazed curiously at Amry and then looked back at each other, puzzled.

"Oh yes," said Amry, "the council could invite us back to live in the forest if they wanted to. They could overthrow that overgrown mosquito in a tutu if they weren't all a bunch of cowards. I'll say it again, if it weren't for them denying our Ancient Magical Creature Status every year, we could return to the Magic Forest and live in our own homes and take our rightful place as the *most* ancient of magical creatures, but alas, yes, alas," Amry raised his pitch dramatically.

"Oh joi de vivre," said Onda sarcastically.

"ALAS folks, we will never be able to return to our rightful home. Prejudice, bigotry, and fear run rampant in those cute little outfits, pointy ears, glittery wings, and jeweled scales."

"Amry, cut it out." whispered Onda. Chev and Coop's baby began to cry, and the new family started to side step away from the camera's view.

"You heard me right folks, we have got to support our tribal leader's efforts in gaining our status back this year. It's now or never I say; now or never."

"Amry, dust off, buddy, you are scaring the entire report away," warned Onda as he threw a pebble, smacking Amry right in his chest.

"Hi-Ho, Hi-Ho, the dwarves have got to go…Oh OUCH! That hurt Onda! Ohhhhhhhhh."

"Sorry about that folks, I got a little carried away. Congratulations are in order to our new parents and their daughter Icab, *great 4 letter segment for a name if I don't say so myself.* For those of you preparing to start a new family, hopefully tonight, you've seen how it's done. They don't call me an information frit for nothing. Well, as I always say, 'Finders Keepers Losers Weepers.' See you tomorrow at 7:59."

Amry smiled sheepishly at the new couple and wished them well and good bye. As he struggled to put his sock back on, he muttered to himself, "Good bye. Good luck. Good riddins' is more like it. I hate doing these reports of the everyday frit. I really hate having to control my mouth and I really, really- dang it this STUPID pink and yellow- who would wear this sock anyway? I am sure I never …Oh dust pan!!" Amry fiddled with his microphone until he pulled it into the sock and waited impatiently behind his disguise for Onda to pack his camera and put his argyle sock back on.

Onda noticed that Amry was appearing impatient as he could see his right foot tapping. He rolled his eyes at his best friend and proceeded to squeeze his body forward to fit back into his footwear. Turning toward the pink and yellow sock with white ducks, Onda lectured the seemingly inanimate object, "You hate me don't you? Why do you always embarrass me with your anger?"

The bright pink object seemed to jump as Amry threw out his arms in rebuttal, "Come on Onda; you know I am right. You know it's the festival of stank-o-rama being a frit. We have no place to call home, none of the frills or perks that come with living in the Magic Forest, and not even the acknowledgement of existence 'cause we don't have AMC status."

"Well," stated Onda with an unseen smile behind his sock, "Your report *reeked* like the pile of vomit by the 'Whip-o-Chunk' at your so-called festival of 'Stank-o-Rama.'"

"At least I don't *look* like that pile of puke," chided Amry. The two friends laughed and headed back towards the TV station.

3

Yo

"Hey snacks!" came a voice from under a dark brown sock with a hole in the heel, bouncing from behind the house where Amry and Onda were standing.

"YO!!!!!!!!!!" screamed Onda and Amry in unison and surprise. "I thought we told you to stay back at the station and label stuff for no reason!" said Amry.

"I ran out of raisins," muffled Yo under his sock as he struggled to move across the street.

All three frits walked swiftly, looking like an upside down, three-legged sack race as they bounded down the overgrown lawns of the unsuspecting, quiet neighborhood.

"Amry, I want to show you what I found," said Yo, who towered over Amry and Onda. The frit stopped to tug on something that was caught in the hole of the heel of the sock he was wearing. He struggled until he fell onto the ground. Amry and Onda had to stop and say the forgetting spell a few times as some cars passed down the street just to avoid being seen while Yo got out of his sock. Amry turned back and reprimanded his tall friend.

"Yo, what is your problem with getting a new sock? You know that this one is causing you problems. It's bad enough that it has a hole in it where you are exposed to the human world, but you can't even get out-of-it to be present in the frit world. Come on!" shouted Amry as he and Onda waited, unsocked, to see Yo's find.

Yo struggled and finally appeared to Amry and Onda, bearing a shiny set of keys with a black and yellow checkerboard pattern on the key chain. "Just look at what I found while I was waiting for you guys to finish the report." Yo shook the keys with pride and smiled wide-eyed.

"Boo hoo," cried Amry as he collected the keys from Yo to examine them. "Dusty doodle, Yo. These are Icab's birth-keys! You know, the ones that her DAD WAS HIDING DURING THE INTERVIEW!!!!" Amry began to bang the key chain back and forth over Yo's dusty chest to emphasize each shouted word. Onda quickly intervened by jumping in between Amry's banging keys and Yo's body, and then whispered into his friend's ear.

"Dust out buddy. You know, Yo is….well he's…okay, he only *visits* his brain from time to time, he doesn't actually *have* one. Let's just re-hide the keys on the way back to the station and we'll give the father a call to let him know what happened. I am sure he'll understand."

Amry gave Yo the evil eye as he handed the keys to Onda. The neighborhood street quieted down as all parents and children had returned from work or school and were comfortably inside eating dinner or playing games. The frits knew that when the sun was setting that it would be safe to take their socks off. All three frits packed their security socks into their respective pockets and bags and then skirted through the lengthy side and backyards of the neighborhood, looking for a place to hide Icab's birth-keys.

Onda stopped at a front porch, which had a medium sized rock lying at the foot of the bottom step. Onda attempted to lift it up to hide the keys under it and found that it was unusually light.

"Amry! Yo! Come check this out. I must be getting stronger; I can lift this huge rock with little or no effort. This is amazing!"

Onda took a closer look at what was oddly printed on the rock and then stamped his feet in disgust as he noticed the words "HIDE-A-KEY" engraved on the bottom. *Oh dust it all*, he thought, *this rock already has a key under it.* Onda waved to Yo and Amry, signaling them to press on for another hiding place.

Yo strolled a little further down the block, looking for a hiding place and a little salvation from the wrath of his friends. After finding a place of use, he backtracked to Amry and Onda for approval. "Hey youfers, I think I have found a great spot for those keys. Follow me." The other two ran to the place where Yo was standing and pointing at a glowing blue lantern hanging over the back door of another house. "I don't think any human will stick their hand in that. It's a great place, right? Did I do a good job?" Yo waited for an opinion either way.

"What is that?" asked Onda.

"More importantly Onda, what is that unelvish noise it is making?" muttered Amry.

Yo answered quickly and confidently, "It's a perfect birth key protector. Look at the blue light. It zaps every time anything comes near it. It's a perfect place to hide the keys." Yo seemed fascinated with the way the mosquito killer quickly stunned the insects as they approached the blue light of death.

"Well, I am glad you pointed out the 'zapping' and the 'anything coming near it' part," said Amry, making quotation marks in the air with his fingers. "Yo, what did you eat for breakfast, your brain?! How are *we* supposed to come near it if nothing else can?" Amry threw his hands up in disgust.

"Just....ooooh, just give me the keys. I'll have Ocus take care of it when we get back to the news room," Amry held out his hands for the keys, while Yo lowered his head and walked out in front of the other two.

"Honestly, Onda, some days I want to take a dust pan to Yo's head and smack him under a rug; but I ...well, I just care what happens to him that's all. It's like everything happens to the poor guy. He is never without trouble." Amry smiled, "Actually, trouble is never without Yo."

"Walk with me Amry," Onda took hold of his best friend's arm with a little force to pull him aside, "Just let it go. There's nothing you can do about it. Yo has been this way since birth. You know that he wasn't born with much use for his own magic. He is forgetful so often that his fritly magic always backfires on him. He makes humans forget the wrong sorts of things, *if* he can get them to forget at all." Amry shrugged knowing that Onda was right and continued walking swiftly over the soft grass of a familiar back yard, just a few feet away from the house where their newsroom was located. They watched as Yo tripped over his long brown sock attempting to get up the steps of the back porch to a big yellow house, while saying the forgetting spell and waving his feather all around as if humans were everywhere, but they weren't.

Onda laughed, "Amry, do you even know how he got that sock of his? It's a hand-me-down from his father. Don't get me wrong. He attempted to get his own sock, like every other frit does during the Security Sock Obtainment Exam in grade school, but it didn't work out as he had planned."

Amry looked at Yo teetering up to the big concrete steps to the back porch of the yellow house and snickered.

Onda continued on, "He was supposed to go to a family's home and make them forget they left one sock in the dryer. Then, he was supposed to take the sock after the family member left the washroom. However, instead of waiting *outside* of the dryer while the human unloaded most of the clothes, Yo decided to wait *inside* the dryer and made the human forget that he had dried the clothes."

Amry mumbled, "Figures."

Onda kept on going, "Sure enough the human forgot and kept re-starting the dryer over and over again. It was weeks before Yo was pulled out of the lint trap. To this day whenever a human plays the 80's hit 'You spin me right round baby,' Yo throws up." Onda held up his nubby-fingered right hand in the swearing position and started to laugh, "It's true."

Amry felt bad about chastising his friend for his actions of late and ran to catch up to apologize to him at the bottom of the back porch steps leading up to the kitchen door of the house.

"I wonder who is on back door duty," Yo thought aloud as he stumbled over the top step and fell onto the porch. Amry helped him up and then took Yo's sock off. Onda had also made it up the back porch steps and was talking to the tiny frit guarding the door, holding it slightly open for the trio to enter.

"Got a good report today?" asked Ford.

"Amry has always got it together," Onda didn't sound so sure of his words but continued the small talk. "We're just heading back to the station to do a little editing."

"Did Amry open his big mouth and start singing the 'Hi-Ho Dwarf' song again?" asked Ford as Onda headed through the kitchen door. Onda peered back onto the back porch, shook his head in embarrassment, and chuckled.

Amry, who was already in the kitchen turned around to check with Ford about the comings and goings of the humans in the house to see if it was safe to scrounge around for dinner.

"Hey, I know we're a little late for dinner, but do you think the dinner-duty frit made Junior forget to close the refrigerator door so we can get in and get some grub?" Ford directed Amry's attention towards the mother of the house, who was yelling from the basement. Amry and his friends immediately put their socks back on and hid behind the trash can next to the fridge, when they heard her voice.

"Child, are you trying to refrigerate the entire suburban area? Ya left the fridge door open again. Please go shut it before I turn into a mom-sicle."

"Oh," said Onda, underneath his sock, "I guess we better get dinner now before Junior heads upstairs and forgets to shut the fridge door again." All three frits peered from around the side of the trashcan to inspect the refrigerator door, which was fortunately, still left open.

Amry pointed to the large appliance and whispered to his friends, "Can youfers stand watch while I grab us some grub?" No one seemed to mind so Amry climbed up the vent at the bottom of the fridge; and Onda said the forgetting spell all the while waving his feather towards the kid stomping up the stairs to get to the kitchen.

Amry's progress to the top of the refrigerator was stopped by Yo tugging on his boots and pleading, "Umm Amry? I want to go in the fridge this time. I can do this. Come on, let me do something for a change. I got this in the sock."

Amry figured this was a harmless enough opportunity for Yo to practice magic and so held his hands out for Yo to get a leg up and head up into the major appliance as he jumped back down. Yo called down from the 2nd shelf, "Well, whoever the dinner duty frit is, he is working overtime. Not only did he make the kid forget to shut the door, he made him forget to eat this perfectly delicious brown, slimy vegetab….."

Amry broke in, "Shh!"

Yo stopped mid-sentence, realizing that the kid who was earlier bounding up the stairs was standing in the kitchen door. The refrigerating frit hid quickly behind the mustard.

"Mom!!!" yelled the kid. "What was I supposed to do again?" The kid shrugged his shoulders and headed for the pantry. Absentmindedly, he opened the pantry closet, looked in for a few minutes, and then closed it again before heading to the fridge. He peered in to check what was available for an after dinner snack and saw that there was a plate of hot dogs and a large bowl of left-over spaghetti. As he reached for the hotdogs, he also reached for the mustard, but not before a tiny feather reached out from behind and Yo whispered these words, "May your forgetfulness be dust upon the heads of all frits present. Forget that you like mustard with your hot dogs. May your forgetfulness be dust upon the heads of all frits present."

Yo fainted from straining so hard to save himself from being noticed by a human, that he didn't even see that Junior took the bowl of spaghetti instead, and left the fridge door open, just as he always did. Junior opened the microwave and set the timer, all the while unaware, or "forgetting" what was right at his feet and what was just in front of his eyes.

Listening to Junior's dinner pop and sizzle, Yo peered out from the open fridge door and feebly held up a thumbs-up sign. Amry and Onda jumped up and down, waving at Yo and shaking their heads back and forth. The kid took his snack out of the microwave and headed out of the kitchen and back downstairs.

As the threatening sound of footsteps faded into the distance, Amry and Onda burst into cheers, "Yo, that was great! I can't believe you got it right that time!"

Yo teetered to the edge of the fridge shelf and fell onto the kitchen floor holding a large stalk of slimy, old celery. "Will this do?" whispered Yo.

Amry and Onda knew Yo wouldn't have brought anything decent out to eat so they crawled into the fridge, grabbed their personal favorites of string cheese and grapes, and hopped back down onto the floor.

"We better get outta here before that mom starts screaming again," said Yo as he clumsily held the celery in his hands and attempted to place his sock over it. They all put their socks back on, ran out of the kitchen into the upstairs dining room, slid across the wood floor until they reached the staircase that led down to the basement living room.

"Look Yo, " whispered Amry, "you may have gotten the spell right that time, but if Junior's mother comes out of the basement unexpectedly, I want you to play dead and be silent." Yo nodded that he understood and the trio carefully climbed down the steps. When the frits approached the fifth or sixth step from the bottom,

Onda pointed to his eyes and then pointed to the living room door. The three frits immediately fell down and made themselves appear limp.

The mother of the house was standing at the bottom of the stairs when she noticed the three socks. She yelled upstairs, "Good gravy child! Can't you take your dirty clothes to the washroom without leaving your socks all over the floor?" She attempted to pick up the pink and yellow sock with white ducks, thinking to herself, "Junior doesn't own a sock like this.", but a feather appeared out from the red and green argyle sock and soon enough the mother decided to leave the sock on the stairs, shaking her head in dismay, and continuing up the stairs in search of her child.

"Whew!" said Amry. "You saved my dusty butt that time."

"Yeh, well, don't expect me to do it every time, I'm not your mother", said Onda as he lifted up the edge of his sock to see if anyone else was coming out of the basement. Onda patted Amry and Yo on the shoulders to let them know it was okay to keep going and the odd-socked creatures climbed down the rest of the stairs and crawled through the half open French doors to the living room.

The family room was large with 2 leather couches on opposite walls and a leather chair on the side. In the back center of the living room was a large television sitting atop an entertainment center with shelves containing a VCR, a DVD player, and a satellite receiver. Behind this entertainment center was where Amry and Onda worked. They were slowly sliding between the large brown leather couch and the wall on the left side of the room to get to the entertainment center, when they heard Junior yell from the hallway. "Mom, what are you talking about?! There aren't any socks on the stairs." He muttered under his breath, "She's losing it for sure", and then headed out the front door to play with his friends.

Amry and his friends crawled out from behind the back edge of the couch and hopped onto the wooden ledge of the entertainment center. Clouds of dust billowed out through the shelving as the friends clambered up a video input/output wire, entering the Fritscovery Channel newsroom behind the television. It was dusty, full of wires, and full of frits getting ready for the evening broadcast.

Every night at 7:59 PM, the Fritscovery news channel would broadcast a short news segment over the public access channel, which is rarely watched by humans, especially at 7:59. This broadcast was meant to keep frits up to date on any activity by their leader, the queen, or even humans, in case their safety was in danger. Amry and his crew were responsible for bringing a special report every night back to the station for editing and broadcasting.

The three frits squeezed past some of their co-workers and climbed up to the back of the VCR shelf, heading for Amry's little corner of workspace.

"Onda, do you have the tape, because we need to get it together quickly and correctly this time or Ocus is gonna fire us for sure." said Amry as he took his sock off and checked some of the bright yellow sticky pad messages left for him on the shelf wall.

"It's in the can, Am. I've got it ready to g…" Onda stopped mid-sentence when he noticed Yo lumbering around, still stuffed in his holey sock. "Yo, take the sock OFF! We are behind the TV now. No human comes back here anyway. Oh, except for the time you unplugged the yellow, white, and red, wires 'cause you were sure the owner didn't set their DVD player up right."

Throwing his warm sock off his head, Yo quickly retorted, "Onda, there could have been a frit in the room when they were reading the DVD player instruction manual. They could have forgotten a step. I told you, I thought the wires looked like they were hooked up incorrectly. I was just trying to help out." Exacerbated, Yo hung his head once again.

"It's alright my little Frit Olay. Now come and help me preview this report so it will be ready for the 7:59. We've only got about fifteen minutes." Onda and Yo moved toward a small digital camera hooked up to the functions of a satellite receiver and a DVD player sitting on top of the VCR. After Onda started the rewind of the tape to preview it he turned to look down to the TV shelf to check on Amry's whereabouts, when he saw him pleading with his boss.

"Come on Ocus, let me do the AMCS report. Let me interview ElCa. Come on, I won't Pledge the whole thing and wipe out our chances of staying on the air. Come on." Amry looked at his boss with puppy-dog eyes.

Ocus put a hand to his balding dust and sighed, "Look. We all know that you admire the human news reporters who give the in depth investigative reports and their opinions, but in *this* society, you are to *deliver* the information, not *comment* on it. Maybe you FORGOT THAT! Half the time I wish I could forget the crud coming out of your mouth." Amry looked puzzled at his boss' derision.

"Well," Ocus continued, "did you know that I got a phone call after your little frit birth interview?" Amry frantically looked around for Onda, caught his eyes and mouthed the words *help me*. Onda, passing one hand over the other and cocking his head to the side, mouthed back, "you're on your own." Realizing that there was no way to escape his superior's wrath, Amry just stared at the ground and began digging his toe into the carpet.

Ocus continued, "Let's just say that the new parents were upset with the *tone* that started the first few moments of their new daughter's life. Something was said about whether or not she would live long *and* happy? Is this what you call well-wishing? Is this the congratulations you would want for *your* first child?"

Ocus bent over a little, trying to catch Amry's evasive eyes, "Heaven forbid you ever have a child. Getting them dressed, bathed, fed, and schooled is a lot of responsibility; not to mention the finances for…"

Amry raised his hand and stopped his boss in mid-sentence, "Focus, Ocus!" He loved saying that. "Look boss, I'll get my act together. You know that I am just excited about the AMCS vote this year. Call me fritriotic or whatever; I can't help it. I came to ask you if I could interview ElCa." Bringing his voice to a fevered pitch, Amry went on, "Our tribal leader could really pull it off this time. I mean, he is such a powerful, persuasive speaker. I think he could get a few votes for our status to be renewed. This might be our year. I'll do whatever it takes. Please give me the assignment to interview ElCa. Please?" Amry bowed his head and pressed his hands together, wincing as he braced for the worst.

"Don't grovel," Ocus said, finally, "I am not the Fairy Queen and besides, it's unbecoming. I'll give you the interview with ElCa. But you must remember that I need the interview ready to go by tomorrow at 7:59. Just clean the dust bunnies off yourself and show a little restraint in your on-air commentaries. Now, get up to the next shelf with Onda and get your 7:59 report for tonight ready. Let's see if you can turn that disaster into a report worth showing in ten, no, eight minutes."

Amry crawled up the cable hooking the TV into the satellite and DVD player and stopped when he reached Onda who had already plugged the pen camera in to download the frit birth interview. It had already rewound and he and Yo were checking each frame of the report, when Amry shoved his way in between them and said "I can't believe he gave it to me!"

"Gave you what?" Onda said as he shoved Amry out of the way so he could finish watching the images on the small pen cam monitor as they downloaded, "a swift kick in the friterry-air? Come look at this to make sure it's the way you want it before I send it over to Saab in broadcasting to plug into the satellite receiver."

Amry began reviewing the film but couldn't help repeating and clarifying his exciting announcement. "No, Onda. He gave me the ElCa interv....WHAT IN THE DUST BUSTER IS THAT?!" Amry said as he pointed to an image on the screen.

"What?!" said Onda, snapping to attention, "I already deleted your 'local crap' segment at the beginning of the report."

Amry spoke loudly and slowly, "Not that. I mean THAT!" Amry pointed to the screen again.

Confused and intrigued, Yo ran over to the monitor, "See what?"

Amry grew louder, "Do you see the incriminating brown sock peering from behind the cab driver's foot as Chev is trying to get his new family out?" Grabbing his dusty coif in despair, Amry gasped, "Holy frito! Do you see the brown sock peering from behind the tow truck in that shot?" Jumping up and down, he continued, "Oh my fritastic fantasy! Did you see the brown sock that just ran in front of the camera like Big Foot?"

Onda and Yo focused all of their attention on each frame that Amry was forwarding and then pointing to. Amry turned to his cameraman, cheeks red and forehead wrinkled, "Onda, surely you saw that. What are you doing when you are filming me -crossword puzzles? Honestly."

He turned and glared at Yo, "And YOU! Why are you in every single shot? How am I going to give this report to Ocus in seven," Amry looked at his watch and threw his hand out, "no, six, minutes?" Wrapping his arms around his head, Amry sat down and buried his head between his knees. He began to breathe in and out very slowly.

Onda patted Amry on the back, "Aww, it's okay, Am. You know I have mad editing skills. I'll work on it right now. I'll fix it. Just sweep it off."

Walking back over toward Yo, he looked sideways at his friend and whispered, "I'd leave the room now if I were you."

Dejected, Yo walked away from his friends to a spot where he could hear the cartoon playing on television. Trying to sound cheery, Yo sang with the TV, "Ohhhhh who lives in a pineapple under the sea?" He sighed and looked down, his bottom lip quivering, "I wish I did."

4

A Little Birdie Told Me

From a round, pink television, in a well-decorated glitzy castle's high tower came Amry's digitized voice piping confidently over the airwaves "Tonight the Fritscovery News Channel brings you up close to a frit birth. We all know that it's not easy ducking the fairy queen's terrible curse…"

"Honestly, Queen Oletta," said a male fairy with pursed lips, tiny glasses, and a weak British accent, "I don't know why you insist on watching these 'fritters' on the tele. They're horribly ilky, roundish, and dirty." He walked into the throne room with an air of assumed sophistication. He fluttered his unusually tall wings to get them into a comfortable position and sat down on a tufted ottoman. He flipped open his lavender flower decoupage note pad and began checking off a 'To Do' list, while watching in disgust as the fabled fairy queen sat intent on watching what he considered frit trash.

The Fritscovery news channel report continued on, "Yes, she will live long. But will she be happy in this nomadic existence forced upon us by the…"

Lance did not like where this report was headed. He liked even less what would happen if the Fairy Queen became disgruntled. He decided to do something about it. He began pacing back and forth across the front of the television so the queen's view of the news was obstructed.

The overly tall, gaunt winged queen shot sparks flying from the edge of her baton-shaped scepter towards her assistant's well manicured bare feet in an effort to get him to move.

It worked. Lance squealed in pain but tried to show no weakness and quickly moved his obstruction of the queen's view. The queen tried her hand at an apology.

"Lance, darling, you can't possibly understand the many facets of the Fairy Queen's duties. It can be quite taxing, and sometimes it requires a little eavesdropping," she said gesturing to the television and listening attentively for news. At the gesture, Lance jumped, expecting another round of sparks from the tips of the queen's acrylic Pepto-Bismol pink colored fingernails.

The TV blared with indignation, "Oh yes, the council could invite us back if they wanted to. They could overthrow that overgrown mosquito in a tutu if they weren't all a bunch of cowards."

Queen Oletta's ears perked up instantly; and she quickly sat upright in her throne. "Did he say what I just heard with my royal ears? Or has the rustling of my OVERGROWN MOSQUITO wings distorted the audio?" The sky of the Magic Forest began to turn black over the queen's castle in synchronization with her swift rising from the throne. She stood at the edge of her chair and tapped her foot angrily as she whipped out and lit a cigarette, "Does my tutu offend?!" Large bolts of lightening streaked across the sky in rhythm to the queen's tapping feet and her sucking in the smoke of the cigarette. Suddenly Queen Oletta unleashed her disapproval of Amry's newscast with a stream of fairy spells at which point many objects in the room became filled with static electricity coming from the streamers that flowed from her scepter. Her assistant, Lance, became quite annoyed with the effect of the static on his perfectly positioned hair.

He separated his wings and flew in a rush to calm the royal. "Queenie, honey, I told you not to watch. You know these dim-witted fritter fratters have never forgiven Your Highness for denying their AMC status. You also know that they blame…" Lance stopped to think before finishing his lecture. *It's not wise to lecture a royal. That's pretty much par for the course. Oh well, I never liked golf anyway.* Lance decided to continue, "Honey, they blame you for being kicked out of their homes in the Magic Kingdom, even though you and I both know that the council voted on that one. You have heard all of this before. This fritter anger is not a surprise. You shouldn't worry yourself; and you must stop smoking." Lance leaned over and took the thin cigarette from the fairy's dainty hands.

The queen shot him a glance of what *in the 'bibbidy bobbidy boo' do you think you are doing.*

Lance recovered by cautiously explaining himself, "I don't mean to overstep my boundaries; but you're gonna turn those beautiful wings yellow."

Ignoring him entirely, the Queen spouted an order, "Lance, fetch my tulle box." He stood perfectly still and stared at Oletta, looking confused at the fact that the queen had anything to do with hammers or screwdrivers.

Queen Oletta dropped her hands from her hips in numb irritation, "Oh for the love of Snow White! You call yourself a fairy?" She lifted her hands and made a square with the index finger and thumb of both hands, "It's the box covered with pink, ballerina tutu material."

"Oh, that one," Lance realized aloud, rolling his eyes as he spun around to fetch from the roll top desk, a box covered in blush pink material. "Shall I look something up for Your Majesty?" he asked expectantly, putting the tip of an extravagantly feathered pen to his mouth.

Queen Oletta seemed put-out by the presumption of Lance asking to go in her tulle box. "Hand that to me at once." The queen snatched the box from Lance's hands and then quickly opened it. She scrambled the contents looking for a small dirty piece of paper and upon finding it, turned to Lance and held it up in his line of sight.

"Your majesty?" said Lance reading the seven digits on the piece of paper and with a slight air of knowing that evil plans were in the making. "I'll fetch the 'little birdie' phone, shall I?" Lance gestured to the mahogany desk with padded lions' feet. The queen nodded in approval. Her assistant grabbed the Austrian crystal encrusted phone shaped like a blue bird and dialed the numbers from the dirty piece of paper and spoke into the birdie phone's tail feathers, "Hello, your leader please."

Lance tapped his pointy shoes slowly and then furiously waiting for a voice at the birdie phone's beak. "Hello? Yes, your majesty requires an odd job. No, it doesn't require *that.* Yes, marshmallows will be given at completion of service. Stop making this so complicated. This is what I want you to do…"

Meanwhile, in the back of the TV at the big yellow house, Amry took his thumb and forefinger and pressed them together over his bulgy nose, trying to relieve the pressure caused by a stress ache. He watched his frit-birth report from his office and shook his head back and forth. *There is no way Ocus is gonna let me keep the interview. There is no way I'm letting Onda edit my reports again. There is no way. There is no way.* Amry pounded his head on the desk a few more times repeating the words, "there is no way". He sat there for what seemed like an inordinate amount of time waiting for the proverbial dust to hit the pan and looked in his desk drawer for a piece of a mirror he kept there to get ready before his nightly reports. *Huh,* he thought. *Looks like I had ink on my thumb. Looks like I have ink on my nose. Can this day get any—Oops, better not think that. There are Accident Gnomes that roam these parts just waiting to hear those fatal exact words.*

Amry looked at the big pocket watch he had found on one of his human-forgetting escapades and noticed that it was 8:59. His report had been broadcast over an hour ago.

Could it be that I have escaped trouble this time around? He lifted his chin and raised his eyebrows in a facial expression full of hope. He looked around for some paper to write out a few questions in preparation for tomorrow's interview with ElCa, the tribal leader. *Why prepare for an interview which may or may not occur at this point?* Amry decided to trudge along and write a few insightful questions in spite of it all. He took out a very small overly sharpened pencil with no eraser and a yellow sticky pad and began to write:

1.As the tribal leader of the frits, what is your primary job/ objective?

2.How did you come to be the tribal leader?

3.Don't you just hate the smug way that Master Dragon Ragule says, "No, to the FRIT" every time our status vote is read over the TV? He says it with smoke billowing through his teeth during the T sound. I hate that. Don't you?

Amry looked back at his list of questions. *Hmm, that last one wasn't really a question was it?* He soon realized that his head was pounding even more than before and he lifted his chin, opened his mouth wide, and stuck his tongue out, hoping to clear his head, or at least force a giggle out to make himself feel better. He was interrupted by a loud tweeting sound coming from the bottom drawer of his desk.

"Did I leave my birdie phone down there; and if so, should I answer it?" Amry questioned himself out loud a few more times before picking up the phone shaped like a bright red cardinal.

"Yesssssss? Speaking. Okay. Yep, I can do that. All right, fine. I'll be there in a few." Amry hung up the phone and placed it in his jacket pocket. He climbed down off his VCR shelf office and down to the bottom of the TV. He sidestepped out of the entertainment center while simultaneously getting into his sock. He peeked out from the side of the blaring TV.

"Guess Junior forgot to turn it off; lucky for me." Amry gloated in his good fortune for the moment and looked around the room to make sure his path of departure was clear. No one was in the room so Amry snuck out from the TV and hopped down to the carpet. He made a quick b-line to the space behind the couch and ran all the way through the French doors, over the wood floors, and out the open basement door.

Amry's phone rang just as he exited the house. "What?!" shouted Amry into the cardinal phone's feathers, while standing in the driveway. "Alright, already, I am rounding the house as we speak. Go sit somewhere and collect dust. I am coming."

Amry slammed the phone shut and put it back in his pocket. He stood still for a few minutes to collect information about his surroundings. He noted that no human was around and made a sigh of relief that he could take the suffocating sock off. The sky was now dark and full of stars. Amry liked to look at them all, when the humans were fast asleep, but there wasn't time, not now, not when fun was to be had.

He ran up the driveway to get to the back of the house and stopped under the porch. Looking around he saw a bright red and green ceramic gnome positioned in the mulch and couldn't help but make fun of it. He stood behind the gnome and held his arms out.

"Funny," he said out loud trying to do his best imitation of a gnome voice by raising the pitch and vibrato of his own. "Humans always get things so wrong about Ancient Magical Creatures. We gnomes are NOT good for the garden. We would just as soon eat you out of house and home than scare the rabbits away. We are NOT this cute and NOT this big."

A voice came from behind a second red and blue gnome, "And NOT likely to sound like a cricket that's swallowed a bumble bee."

Amry jumped out from behind the concrete gnome and approached the voice coming from behind the second gnome. The voice was still talking.

"And most people don't know this, but I am secretly in love with Amry the frit. He is the best journalist on the Public Access channel at 7:59. No one does interviews like he does. And as a gnome, I know it's forbidden, but those eyes, those teeth, that hair…"

Amry grabbed the brown-jacketed unusually shorthaired frit from behind the gnome and put him in a playful chokehold.

5

Tang's Bangs

"Aww come on Amry, you wouldn't hurt a secret admirer, would ya?" The frit tried to wrestle out of Amry's chokehold but to no avail. Amry held onto the dusty hair of the frit and pulled him even closer.

"Tang, you're lucky I still like you or instead of a secret admirer, you would be an unsolved mystery." Amry let go of the frit's hair, which made him fall to the ground and they both began to laugh.

Tang put out his hands for Amry to help pick him up and then threw his right arm over Amry's shoulders to quickly lead him through the side yard to a row of fir trees that separated Amry's residence with its neighbor.

"Am, I think you are in need of some good old fashion frit-fun. Come away with me."

"What makes you say that? Oh wait, let me guess? You saw the 7:59?" Amry waited for Tang's retort.

Tang responded, "You know I only watch the REAL news." Amry put his right hand into action pretending to stab himself in the heart with a knife.

"Just come on. You'll like this, plus, I had my hair cut just for tonight so I have a reason to grow it all back. Come on, let's go." Tang pointed his stubby fore-finger towards the next backyard and started running. Amry followed until Tang reached a rain spout at the bottom of a gutter at the corner of the next house.

Catching his breath, Tang stuttered "L-l-listen." Amry eyed Tang wondering what he was up to now. Then Amry remembered what had occurred at this very spot so many times before. They were standing at the corner of Mr. Paul's garage.

He shook his head emphatically, "Nope. Not this time. You are gonna get us in trouble with ElCa. We are not supposed to cause so much trouble as to cause a human to believe they are coming down with a serious mental disorder."

Tang shrugged his shoulders, "What ElCa don't know won't hurt him; besides, Mr. Paul has never uttered out loud that he thinks he's going crazy, although I've heard his wife say it a couple of times."

Amry just hung his head and shook it back and forth all the while mouthing the words *no, no, no*.

Convinced that Amry would at least watch as he embarked on his first frit magic escapade for the evening, Tang donned his mischief making face.

"Look, Mr. Paul just works on motorcycles as a hobby. It's not like it's his job. No one is going to get mad at him if he takes too long to install a new exhaust system. You know you want to see this."

Amry asked Tang if he was going to wear his sock or go "full-frit" (which means uncovered). Tang assured Amry that he knew the way and had never been seen before. So, Amry gave in with a thumb's up sign and peered around the corner of the house as Tang lightly crept up to the open garage door.

Mr. Paul sat in his garage filled with an endless supply of small and large boxes of motorcycle parts which looked as if they had been shipped back and forth to one address or another at least eight times. He sat there calculating his next several steps to perform on the installment of the new exhaust for the motorcycle. He tried to determine what tools he would need in advance, wondering how he could avoid turning circles in the garage looking for stuff while trying to do his work at the same time.

Tang waited until Mr. Paul walked to the other end of the garage grabbing this tool and that tool before he tiptoed right next to the box of parts that were needed for the installment. Tang looked inside the box by standing on his tiptoes and stretching up to the edge of the box. "*Rats! The parts aren't in the box.*" Tang whispered to himself in dismay.

However, he soon realized that his luck had not run out yet when he noticed that Mr. Paul had carefully laid each piece to be installed in a row parallel to the motorcycle so that when he needed the next piece, it would be right there. Tang thought that this set up was even better.

He hid behind the box and waited for Mr. Paul to return with the tools, counting the pieces, big and small, as they sat there in the row. There were twenty-nine pieces in all. They ranged from nuts and bolts, to parts that Tang did not know the name of. He decided to go with part number fifteen. He noticed that after part fifteen, all the rest of the parts were placed over that one. If Mr. Paul forgot to put the fifteenth part on, he would have to dismantle the entire set-up and start all over again.

Mr. Paul sat by the motorcycle, unaware of Tang's position and began with part number one. Tang waited and waited until part number fourteen was being installed. Tang uttered the spell, "May your forgetfulness be dust upon the heads of all frits present. Forget to install part number 15. May your forgetfulness be dust upon the heads of all frits present." Tang took out a beautiful jet-black feather and waved his words towards the unsuspecting mechanic.

Tang peered from the side of the box to see if Amry was still watching from the corner of the garage door, by the drain spout. He noticed that Amry's brown leather boots could still be seen on the ground; and feeling assured that his efforts would not go unnoticed, he turned back around to see Mr. Paul had skipped part fifteen and went straight on to part sixteen.

"Mission accomplished," whispered Tang as he snuck back out of the garage door and back to the side of the house.

"Amry, just wait and watch. This is gonna be great." Tang flicked his bangs to show how one side was growing longer than the next. Amry flicked his bangs back to show that his hair was growing as well and that Tang's spell must have worked its magic.

As the night wore on, they sat in the grass playing with twigs and rocks, waiting for any sign that Mr. Paul was going to "lose it".

Tang got up and peeked into the garage. "He's just getting up now."

Tang began to give Amry the "play-by-play", *"He is admiring his work. He is tugging on everything to see if it's all in place and securely fastened. Umpp. He feels a weak spot. He looks puzzled."* Tang's voice showed increased anticipation with every sentence. Tang continued, "Here it comes. Wait for the fireworks, Wait. Wait. Three, two, one."

Mr. Paul yelled at the top of his lungs, "GOOD GRACIOUS ALMIGHTY AND A HALF!!!!!!!!" He picked up the small nut and rubbed it between his thumb and forefinger and then stuck it between his front teeth. He bit down on it hard and then put it in his pocket.

"Petunia!!!!!!!!!!" he yelled. "Petunia, get down here. It's happening again. Pehhhhh, toooon, yaaaaaaaaaa!!!" He screamed at the top of his lungs to get his wife's attention.

"WHHHHHHHHHHHHHHHHHHHHHHAAAAAA AAAAAAAAAATTTTT!", she screamed back from the top of the staircase that led from the kitchen to the garage. She waited for a response from her husband.

Mr. Paul walked to the top of the stairs and said, "It's happening again."

Petunia rolled her eyes and said, "What is happening again?"

"Tooney, honey, you know exactly what is happening. I am forgetting the dumbest of things. I forgot to put the nut on the bolt in the very middle of my exhaust installation and now I am going to have to take the whole thing apart and start all over again." Mr. Paul wiped his brow and looked up at his wife for any kind of sympathy.

"Darling husband, do what you have to do. My rollers are in and I am going to bed in 5 minutes, and DON'T think I'll wait up for you." Petunia walked back up the stairs and back into the kitchen.

After having the laugh of a lifetime, the two old friends left the side of Mr. Paul's house and roamed the empty neighborhood sidewalks, frittering around causing boyfriends to forget what driveways to drop their girlfriends off, cats to forget what house they actually got fed at, and many a father to forget to turn the porch light off.

When the sun lit up the sky enough to see, Tang paused at the edge of the curb of the sidewalk and pointed at the house to the right of where Amry lived.

"Remember this place?" asked Tang as he pushed Amry to take a look in the back yard of the house. They both put on their socks in case anyone was up this early and it was a good thing too because sure enough there was a man sowing a small garden in his backyard. The garden was contained by chicken wire and a homemade wooden gate. Amry and Tang crouched down behind a small shrub next to the garden fence and Tang told Amry of his plan.

"Remember Farmer Clark?" Tang inquired of his friend. Amry assured Tang that he remembered the gardener. "Okay, you know the plan right?" Tang looked for Amry's consent.

Amry stared at the unaware farmer digging and carefully placing the seeds in little holes in each carefully hoed row. "Tang, you are merciless. Can't you leave this guy alone? How many times have you pulled this stunt?"

Tang retorted, "I don't know the number; but let's just say it's about to be x+1." Tang's mischievous facial expression was enough to bring a smile to Amry's faces as he asked Tang about the next move.

"Alright then, the plan is the same as before?" Amry was unsure if Tang had changed up his repertoire.

Tang shook his head in confusion at how Amry could forget.

"Yep. We basically stand right behind the large wooden post of the gate and make him forget to put a seed in each of the holes. He will then cover the holes with dirt. By three weeks, that whole row will be empty." Tang seemed quite pleased with his plan.

"Wait a minute, I thought we were gonna make him forget what type of seed he was supposed to plant in each row. Do you remember the time we did that; and he planted the chrysanthemums in the gated garden and the six foot corn in his front yard? Classic, buddy, classic." Amry chuckled at the visual image this memory brought back to him.

Tang rubbed his jaw, watched the farmer, and pondered a few seconds as to which course of action to take. Tang raised his finger in an "AHA!" position. "I've got a new plan. You know how he always keeps Popsicle sticks in his left hand to mark the rows in which he has planted a seed?" Amry nodded yes. "Okay, here's what we do. We make him forget which hand he is using to plant with and which hand he is using to mark with. I wonder what sprouts from the ground if you plant a Popsicle stick?"

Amry shook his head emphatically, "Oh yes. This is gonna be good." The two sock-less frits inched their way across the back yard. They shimmied behind some side yard shrubs until they crossed into Farmer Clark's back yard. They avoided a robin eyeing them suspiciously.

"Shoo!" whispered Tang as they passed by the bird sitting in the lower branches of a shrub right by the garden gate.

Tang turned to Amry, "Why don't you do it this time? Your dust could use some more growing. Come on."

Amry took off his sock and wobbled his neck side to side to stretch his magic making muscles. This was a sign to Tang that Amry was going to take him up on his offer. He brushed both of his hands together back and forth many times in a vain attempt to warm up his magic power and whispered the forgetting spell, "May your forgetfulness be dust upon the heads of all frits present. Forget which hand to use while sowing your seeds. May your forgetfulness be dust upon the heads of all frits present."

At the end of his utterance, Amry took the bird feather from his pocket and whisked his words towards Farmer Clark. The gardener never even noticed that he changed hands with which to put things into the holes of the rows in his garden. Amry and Tang peered around the garden gate just in time to see Farmer Clark plant his very first Popsicle stick.

Tang flicked his now evenly growing bangs at his friend and Amry flicked his evenly growing bangs back.

"I definitely needed that," said Amry.

Tang and Amry, satisfied with their forgetfulness escapades headed for the sidewalk and back to the TV station. Amry chuckled to himself and turned to Tang, "You know, you always make me feel better even if it is at the expense of others. One day, these mischievous escapades are going to come back to haunt us." Tang nodded in agreement and turned to Amry appearing a little more serious than usual.

"Look, I wanted to ask you a question, since you're sort of a know it all." Tang appeared a little distressed. He pulled on one of his thumbs nervously waiting for Amry to acknowledge that he was listening.

"You say something buddy?" Amry obviously wasn't listening to Tang while he was braiding his newly grown bangs. "Is this a good look for television? How 'bout I wear my dust like this?"

Amry soon noticed that Tang was intent on him paying attention to a new turn in the conversation. "What?" Amry asked.

Tang stopped pulling on his thumb and began twirling his newly grown bangs, "See Am, I have been offered quite a nice position in a new firm, as it were."

"Firm?" Amry looked confused and surprised. "Tang we don't have lawyers in the frit world. Are you watching that human show

Law and Order again? I told you the television would rot your brain, I should know. I am a complete idiot for working for a TV station for the last two years, or for having Onda and Yo tag along on my TV reports." Amry was quite proud of that twisted remark.

Tang's facial expression did not change. "Okay, well maybe I don't know what the organization is called as a group; but I have been offered a position just the same, and I want to talk to you about it." Tang reached for Amry's shoulders to stop him from kicking every tiny pebble his boots hit across the sidewalk.

Tang stepped up close to Amry and pulled on his leather vest. Amry slow down, I need to talk to you." Amry nearly fell backwards onto Tang and almost knocked him over. Tang caught himself and avoided falling.

"Spill it buddy. What is this job? Are you gonna take it? Why are you being so cryptic?" Amry's interest in Tang's career opportunity became instantly overbearing.

"Well you don't have to interview me; I just want to know what you think." Tang's remark was defensive and he jogged over to the side yard of the house in which the Fritscovery News Channel resided, and then leaned on the garden hose spout under the porch.

"Just tell me *exactly* what's on your mind." Amry paid just the right amount of attention this time and waited for his friend to collect his thoughts. He sat down on the hexagonal shaped head of the sprinkler, waiting.

"Okay, the Key-pers have asked me to join their organization." Tang winced and hid under a few tangled knots of the water hose.

"The WHAT?! The Key-pers? Tang, NO! No, No No! You know you can't join them." Amry swept back a few loops of the water hose with his hands to find where Tang was hiding.

Tang ran out from behind the hose and hid behind one of the gnomes where he started the adventures the previous evening under the porch. "Aww Am, I knew you'd be mad at me." Tang looked at Amry who was nodding yes and giving the *You knew I would be mad* face.

"I need this Amry. Not all Key-pers are bad. Not everything they do is bad for the frit community. It's what I am good at and, you know it." Tang spoke with a little indignation.

Amry knew it would be pointless to go on arguing with Tang once he'd made up his mind. "Fine Tang, do what you want. It's your life; but when they steal your birth keys and threaten to have your birth car owner find them because you won't do what they say anymore, well, just don't come crying to me. One day you will find out that the organization is corrupt and they won't, I repeat, *won't* let you leave."

Amry kicked the red boots of the ceramic gnome that Tang was hiding behind. Amry decided to say one thing more as he noticed Tang walking out from behind the gnome and back out to the tree in the side yard. "Tang, just think about it, okay?" Amry looked in the dew-spattered grass for his friend but in vain. Tang was already down the side yard and too far away to hear Amry's plea.

Amry shuffled to the front door. *Good thing Mister forgot to shut the front door or I'd be out here arguing with Tang all morning.* Amry wanted to say "Could this get any worse" once again, but he knew better. *Better not invite bad luck in; I've got enough of that on my plate.* He wedged himself through the crack in the basement door, waved to Niss, the night shift door duty frit who was changing guard with Ishi on day shift, and headed to his usual resting place in the foyer shoe closet. *I'll get to the bottom of this Key-per thing once and for all. Tang knows this is wrong. I should've never gone out tonight. Am I forgetting something? I think I am forgetting something?* Amry's mind raced until it was numb and he fell asleep in a large brown leather shoe.

6

Making Up

A small frit clothed in a simple, but pretty, tan suede jumper yelled into the open shoe closet, "Wake-up sunshine!"

Amry positioned his newly grown dusty hair out of the shoe to avoid stepping on it and then pulled himself out. After he squinted in the mid-morning sunlight coming through the foyer windows and shining into the shoe closet his eyes rested on his friend, Olet, who was beaming with her usual morning happiness, violet grey dusty hair, and her word feather dangling in her right ear. She stood there staring at Amry dangerously swinging her make-up kit.

"Already?" asked Amry as if he 'already' knew the answer.

"Am, you know your hair always grows after a night on the prowl with Tang. I can't let you go on your big interview with ElCa looking like this." Olet swung her make-up bag towards Amry, knocking him back into his resting shoe. Amry placed both hands in front of him in the STOP position. Olet took a few steps back and motioned for Amry to get up and go to the box of baby wipes in the purse on the floor of the shoe closet.

"Did you say the interview was today? That can't be right?" Amry yawned wide and held his chubby fingered hand over his mouth to prevent potentially hazardous smells emanating out of it. He scratched his scalp. Dusty hair was always so itchy in the morning. *Maybe it's the shoe,* he thought as he excused himself for a moment to get some wipes to rinse out his mouth and to go behind the overcoat to straighten his clothing.

"Come on, I've got another job besides being at your beck and call you know." Olet banged on her make-up box in an effort to get Amry's attention from behind a large black overcoat hanging in the back of the closet.

"I'm coming." Amry moved the bottom of the overcoat aside and nearly tripped on his long dusty hair before he centered himself again and sat down on the heel of an overturned clog.

Olet began to tease up the dust of Amry's hair, which had become quite flat as Amry slept in the shoe. "You've got shoe-hair again. What did I tell you about putting it in a cap of some kind?" Olet pulled out an extra cap, which resembled a gnome's pointy hat.

"Are you crazy? I'm not wearing one of those. It will make me look like a giant gnome and I like my dust the way it is, thank-you." Amry smiled at his chastisement to Olet. She pulled on his hair a little harder in retaliation to his prejudice and made up her mind to add make-up to his face before cutting his hair like she did every morning before a big interview. She applied a few dabs of powdered clay to his face.

"You always seem so washed out on camera. Maybe if you didn't go out every night, you might get more sleep." Olet knew she was talking to a brick wall in this regard.

Amry reached for Olet's case and picked up a small shard of mirror and held it up. "That's just great. How many times do I have to threaten you? I'm gonna tell Wind and Star that, if you don't stop painting me up like an Oompa Loompa, I'm gonna hire a new make-up artist." Amry grabbed what looked like half a q-tip and began swabbing off most of the clay powder applied to his face.

Olet watched in disgust as Amry completely ruined her efforts to make him appear reasonable in front of the camera. "Fine! This is only the most important interview *you* will ever get to do, so look like a troll for all I care." Olet closed her make-up kit with a slam and hopped off of the high heel pump she was standing on to do Amry's hair and then bounded out of the shoe closet door.

"You know, you could just say, 'thank-you'. Honestly, I don't know why I keep you on as a client. And you can forget about me cutting your dust now. You look more like an electrocuted elf than an Oompa Loompa, anyway. I have half a mind to..." Olet's voice trailed off as she passed through the crack in the front door.

Well that was the quickest I have ever gotten rid of her. Amry smiled at his ability to dismiss unwanted, yet necessary, evils. *Hmm, I wonder if Yo and Onda are at the TV station.* He weaved in and out of the maze of shoes that littered the closet floor and peeked out of the large cracked opening of the closet door.

"Dust it all, the ElCa interview is today and I have no idea what to ask him. I don't even know what order to ask the questions I don't have written, or where to go to ask him the questions in the order that

I don't have them." Amry shuffled through the open French doors to the living room.

"Hey Am." A well-dressed frit waved Amry on through the open French doors.

"How is door duty Ishi?" Amry always enjoyed a pleasant greeting in the morning and always made time for polite chitchat.

"Same-o, Same-o Amry. Hey, I heard you got the ElCa interview. Is that today?"

Ishi's question was harmless enough but Amry wondered if every one in the 7:59 Fritscovery Newsroom was trying to make today difficult, all starting with his make-up artist, Olet.

"Yeah, that's today. Did Olet do a good job making me look like an idiot, 'cause heaven knows I can do that today, all by myself."

Ishi looked a little confused at Amry's remarks and simply grinned as he waved Amry through the open doors to the living room. Amry slid between the living room wall and the brown leather couch as he always did on his way to the Fritscovery News Channel station behind the TV. His reluctance to face his crew and his boss after his disappointment with the editing and the airing of his report last night slowed his climbing up the shelves to his office on the VCR shelf. As he reached the second shelf he took a deep sobering breath hoping this would calm him down before the array of questions and derogatory comments about his report would surely start flying; but, they didn't.

"Amry are you ready? Today is the big day." a co-worker of Amry's shouted from behind a small makeshift cubicle.

"Hey Am, good luck today!" yelled another TV anchorman from around the corner. Amry started to think that his luck was turning around until he turned the corner to go to his office.

"Finally!" someone screamed from behind Amry's desk.

"You finally decide to show up for work. If it were me, I would have come in early, cleaned out my desk, and left before my boss showed up. I had the misfortune of watching an *unedited* version of your 'Happy Birthday Baby' report last night."

Amry watched in horror as his boss paced his office talking to the floor and talking to Amry at the same time. "Sir, I can explain." Amry walked over to the small coke bottle cap, tried to sit down, and tried to twist his dust-hair into a bun held in place by a pencil nub.

"Don't you have an interview to prepare for?" Ocus shifted his attention from the floor to Amry's weary eyes.

"Shouldn't you appear nervous and in excruciating pain knowing that I am letting you keep the biggest interview of your unnatural born life?" Ocus walked towards Amry in an attempt to show superiority and contempt at the same time. "Shouldn't you appear less like an old lady with a bun and more like a top notch reporter? I am positive that I sent Olet to the shoe closet this morning. She is getting too new fashioned if you ask me. You look like you just got up. Be grateful, be prepared, and GET A HAIR CUT."

Amry stammered, "I am grateful Ocus, sir, I am preparing as we speak. I am leaving sir, honest." Amry leaped over his boss who was leaving and sprinted to his own desk to shuffle through his papers to find the set of questions he had starting writing the night before. *Okay, Ocus is gonna let me do this. I cannot let him down. I have to get my self together. Think, Amry, think.*

Amry sat at his desk with a facial expression of what seemed to be great thought and what brought Onda, who was just showing up to work as well, to say, "If you stress out over this interview before it has begun, you'll get mattes in your dust and that does *not* look good on camera, nor does your present state of hair." Onda squished his face into one of disdain at Amry's new hairdo with a twist of pencil.

"Back out, Onda!" said Amry as he stared at his last night's list of questions. "Onda, I'm serious, get out. I don't want to be a troll, but I have to have time for myself. I must get these questions written. I don't even have a place to interview ElCa. Wait, I haven't even called him to set up the time for the interview." Onda watched Amry slowly rise from his desk stool, grab his pink sock, and then leap down from the second shelf to the first and then onto the floor behind the TV. Amry quickly yelled back instructions to his cameraman.

"Onda meet me at the Wind Star Twin Style Salon in 1 hour. Don't bring Yo!" Amry quickly exited through the left corner of the entertainment center, which met up with a large book shelf which led to another entrance behind a small leather love seat.

Amry approached the edge of the love seat and listened. He definitely thought he heard human activity. He immediately placed his pink sock on. *Hmmmf. This had better work. They always know what to do and I definitely need to apologize. Maybe they'll throw in a sauna treatment for the cause.* Amry's hopes bounced in his head as he covered himself, and carefully crawled over the linoleum to the concrete floor of the washroom in the basement adjoining the living room.

7

Fashionably Late and Later

Amry stepped slowly and lightly into the washroom. One wrong move and he'd be in the dryer, or worse, the washer, for eternity. He slowly lifted up the bottom right edge of his sock to see if he could safely walk around the washroom without it. His eyes saw the dryer, utility sink, washer, clothes hangers, and no sign of Mrs., Mister, or Junior.

Quietly, he took off his sock, folded it as compactly as possible, and shoved it into the satchel he was wearing across his chest. As he approached the space between the washer and the dryer, he thought, *no need to be cautious this is frit territory, for now at least.*

The rolling drum of the dryer and fresh sprits of cold water from the lid of the washer always soothed him. He walked to the dark space behind the dryer only to find it lit-up with frit hustle, bustle, and style. As he walked through a hanging dryer sheet doubling as an entryway and an air-freshener, he called out for the ones who just might be able to get him out of a jam.

"Wind, Star, your walk-in, never calls for an appointment, never takes care of his hair, celebrity is here. HELP!!!!!"

Two small, very fashionable, heavily made-upped, and accessorized beyond belief identical twin fritlies approached the bewildered and completely strained reporter.

"Darling little fuzz ball, we knew you'd be coming."

Wind, the twin who wore flowing skirts and her hair in the perpetual wind blown look, placed her arms around Amry and squeezed him tight. She was immediately pried from Amry by the bejeweled hands of her very "glam" twin, Star.

"Amry, my little dryer lint, don't let my sister drool all over you like that, it's bad for the skin." Star shot her airy sister a toothy grin of *I'm only kidding* as she led Amry to sit down on an overturned cup that belonged to an empty bottle of laundry detergent.

"Let's see this disastrous hairdo you have whipped up today." Star began tugging at Amry's long locks of dust that were half cut by Olet.

Amry winced and whined a little as Star attempted to shape his hair with a small comb. To escape his pain, he looked at what he always thought was beautiful. He peered over his shoulder for a moment and caught a glimpse of Olet who had just returned from Amry yelling at her and was now helping another customer at her workstation.

Star noticed that she was cutting Amry's hair crooked because his head was "somewhere else", so she whispered to Amry, "Child, I know you don't like her, but she's cast an awful forgetting charm over herself about that very fact. Why don't you give her a chance every now and then?" Amry shrugged and let Star go back to tending his hair.

Star's twin sister, Wind, slid across the dryer lint and dust covered floor and handed what looked like a tiny wig to her sister. Wind whispered to her sister that they were having a sale on the "Multi colored Lint weave" and that this particular light lavender colored wig might work well to cover Amry's "shoe-hair". Star shooed Wind off of her ear.

Wind decided to take matters into her own hands. "Amry, bunny honey, how 'bout if Star shaves all this matted up dust off your head and gives you a perfectly shaped hair cut out of this freshly obtained dryer lint. It's a great color and they are on sale. Waddya say?" Wind pushed Star out of the way in an effort to fit the wig over Amry's hair to give him an idea of what it would look like.

Star elbowed her way back into the position to finish smoothing out Amry's hair. "Alright Miss Buttinski, I will handle this all by my little self. Amry is a celebrity and he needs a *star* to shed some light on his dust disaster." Star waited for her sister to put the wig back on the counter and then turned her attention back onto Amry.

"Sweepie pie, let's just give you a nice, albeit possibly painful, hair cut and send you on your way to that report you are gonna do with ElCa."

Star began to tug at his hair, once more, to finish removing the mattes and the knots of dust. Amry appeared to be going through some discomfort with the wincing of his eyes and small yelps that came out of his mouth every so often. Star eventually whipped out her crystal encrusted cutting scissors and worked effortlessly to give him a flawless new hairdo.

She handed Amry the mirror to look at the back of his hair but instead, he noticed that his make-up artist, Olet, was at her workstation cleaning up dust clippings and wiping down her chair. He was a little surprised a moment later to find Olet staring back at him. She noticed him looking too and pounded her fist into the air to show her lingering anger towards Amry's grumpiness that morning.

Star interrupted this awkward moment with her usual nosiness. "Everyone is buzzing about this interview you are going to air tonight. I can't wait. I am so excited for you, not to mention you are gonna look good doing it."

Amry finally stopped looking at Olet and looked at his new hair style and was pleased. He faced Star and decided that now would be a good time to ask for some assistance in the matter of his big interview. "Star, how about I ask you and your sister what *you* would ask the tribal leader if you were doing the interview?"

Wind was standing nearby and, just as nosy as her twin sister, scurried back over to Star's hair cutting station and leaned on her sister's shoulder waiting for her twin's answer and for her turn at answering Amry's question as well.

He knew these twins well enough to know that they would be willing to offer their advice as any hair stylist of any species would be. "Okay, wait, let me clarify, I don't mean what kind of toothpaste does he use or who does his dust, but you know, be serious." Amry waited for the twins to think and give him some good questions to use.

Wind was the first to offer her idea, "Child, I have been dying to know how old he is. You know he has got to be older than seven. Does that come with the territory of being the tribal leader? Do you get to live longer, and if so, do you age slower? I mean, this could be an ancient beauty secret. I might wanna be tribal leader next, you know." Wind seemed pleased with her clever question and looked for agreement from her sister.

Amry shrugged his shoulders and spun around to face Star who seemed lost in thought. She closed one eye, looked up to the ceiling of the washroom and said, "Oh, this is too easy Am. I want to know, no, I have been dying to find out what style is in season at the Fairy Castle. Queen Oletta knows how to dress, decorate, and accessorize."

Wind, butted in again, "Ooh, you know that girl has always got it together; and since our kind has been banned from the Magic Forest, we never get to see the trend that she sets every year. I think that's why my fashion sense is not what it could be.

Star chuckled and nodded her head "yes" seeming to agree that her sister's sense of style was definitely off.

Wind nudged Star to stop laughing and continued to prod Amry. "Will you be interviewing ElCa today while he is at the Ancient Magical Creature Council at the castle or at the Great Oak? Maybe you could sneak a peek at the queen?" Both girls giggled and shuddered at the glee they would feel to get a glimpse of the Queen on the television.

Amry's eyes lit up. That was it. He knew what to ask and where to ask it. "Girls, you are marvelous. Those are great questions. Furthermore, I will buy one of those multi-colored lint wigs. I have a friend whose dust has grown so thin that this might be of use to him."

Wind placed the soft lavender colored dryer lint wig in Amry's hands and he handed Wind a tiny pearl bead he had kept in his satchel for just such an occasion. Feeling much better and prepared to take on this momentous task, Amry popped up out of the make-shift chair, passed through the dryer tissue curtain door, and waved goodbye to the twins.

He gave a wave over his head and shouted, "Olet, I am sorry about this morning. I did act like a troll." Amry ran out of the door not waiting Olet's response and nearly bowled over Onda who was just entering the space between the dryer and the washer.

"Onda, perfect timing. Do you have your gear with you? We have got to catch ElCa at the right moment." Amry scrambled to gather the wig and himself up off the concrete floor and to pick his friend up.

"Dust it Am, you're not Ocus. I don't need you to boss me around. Are you ever gonna let up or are you gonna be a bossy grumpy troll all morning?" Onda seemed a little put out by Amry's actions as of late and was unwilling to jump at Amry's commands until he started showing a little courtesy and respect.

Amry hung his head and spoke softly, "I didn't mean to be cantankerous last night. I, well, the big interview was, *is*, hanging in the balance; and I wanted or *still want* everything to go right. You forgive me right? Or do you need ElCa to put a forget spell on you to erase such a horrible memory?" Onda didn't answer and Amry didn't expect him too. He knew that his best friend would forgive him no matter what kind of mood he was in.

So, he picked his cameraman up off of the concrete floor and both frits decided to put their socks on preparing to sneak out the garage door, left open, once again, by Junior.

At the bottom of the driveway, now wearing his pink and white duck sock and waving his spell feather around finishing up the forgetting charm, he realized that Onda was still back at the garage door trying to get his sock fully over him and the camera gear.

"Hurry up, Onda" he yelled in an attempt to get his friend to move a little faster.

"I'm coming your majesty." Onda scooped up all his valuables, which had accidentally fallen out of his large cloth satchel, which resembled a sling for holding babies, the first time he tried to put his sock on. He managed the second time to fit his sock over his belongings and body and yelled back, "Where are we going anyway? Why do you always wait till the last minute to tell me anything?"

Amry stopped in his tracks, waiting for him to catch up. "Okay, here's what we are going to do. ElCa knows we are doing an interview today, but I have yet to tell him where to meet us. I am going to make it a surprise interview but an investigative interview at the same time. This isn't just about ElCa, it's about all the creatures who have been put down on account of the queen and her dumb ole "status council". We are going straight to the Great Oak; you know the entrance to the Magic Forest. Maybe we can get in and meet ElCa as he is coming out of the council meeting. Maybe we can interview some of the other magical creatures."

Onda eyes opened his mouth to say "but Amry."

But Amry stopped Onda short and continued, "Don't worry Onda." Amry looked at his pocket watch he had removed from his desk drawer. "Ooh, it is almost noon. We had better get going or we will definitely be late to do the interview and have time to *really* edit the report this time."

As the two frit friends trotted down the driveway wearing their socks, Onda whispered to Amry, "Nice wig ya got there."

"I dropped that on the floor? Oh. That's a present for someone I know."

"Right. That's what they all say." laughed Onda as they traveled one block down the sidewalk and then turned right at a community playground with an un-mowed meadow right next to it with a large oak in the center.

I hope we're not too late, thought Amry.

8

The Chance Meeting

The neighborhood playground was a rectangular shaped mulched area with two swing sets, one wooden fort tower, and one metal jungle gym. The wooden picnic tables with benches were available for parents to sit on while watching their kids play. Off to the left and behind the benches was a small meadow with a large oak tree and a log in the center of the field. The oak tree had very large leaves flapping in the gentle breeze. And the large hole in the trunk of the tree was hollowed out by fairy magic, to be sure.

This was no ordinary tree. The tree led from the human world to the Magic Forest. Most human children could tell you that the Magic Forest is where most magical creatures reside, but they couldn't tell you how to get there. There is only one way and it was through the Great Oak.

However, you could only enter through the magic oak if you knew the password. All frits, except for their leader, were not allowed to have the password to pass through the oak since Queen Oletta and the Magical Creature Council had revoked their Magical Creature Status centuries ago. So, Amry and Onda tried their hand at the guessing game.

They carefully approached the opening of the tree. There were three human children playing around the swings and the jungle gym; but they were too engrossed in a game of tag to notice two socks walking in the high grass to the tree, besides, Amry and Onda had already said the forgetting spell a few times.

After they entered the spacious hole in the trunk of the oak tree and took their socks off, Amry raised his hands and whispered, "Little pig, little pig, let me in." Nothing but a cricket chirp interrupted the silence after his chant.

Onda pushed Amry over and asked if he could try. As he moved his hands in a sweeping motion from left to right he cried in a loud booming voice, "OPEN SESAME!" The two friends waited in silence as a few leaves from the oak tree rustled in the breeze. "Dust it all." Onda exclaimed. He now knew that human TV shows must be inaccurate; they always showed that those words worked in opening magic doors.

Amry tried again, this time with the only real spell he knew. "May your forgetfulness be dust upon the heads of all frits present. Forget your concealment spell. May your forgetfulness be dust upon the heads of all frits present." Amry and Onda both took their word feathers and waved the words from Amry's spell towards the opening of the oak tree.

Nothing happened.

Amry and Onda looked at each other and were about to mutually give up, until they noticed that each other's bangs were growing. Amry took a look around the cavernous opening of the tree and saw what he thought was a tiny gnome with an official badge reading "Ian".

The gnome seemed to be screaming and jumping up and down. They leaned down to the gnome to hear what was being said with a high pitch sing song voice.

"What the…!" he screamed with the voice of a hummingbird as he stomped all around the base of the tree trunk kicking up dirt all around him.

"Whoa Am, what did you do?" Onda's eyes opened wide to see the gnome scramble to the back dark corner inside the oak trunk.

"Lucky guess." Amry smiled as he thought of what luck just fell before him. Amry leaned down to the trunk floor to get a better look at the gnome and ask a few questions. The gnome was indeed a sight to behold for the frits who rarely glimpsed magical creatures these days. He had curly red hair and wore green short pants, a yellow wool tunic, and dark green boots. Amry thought it looked very green and very tailored which suited the little guy with the nametag.

Amry began his interrogation, "Hi, um Ian is it? I didn't mean to startle you. I just wanted to visit our leader who is at an AMCS meeting in the Magic Forest. I have a 'Press Pass'. Do you know how to get in?" Amry held up what appeared to be an official photo ID with his name and the words "Press Pass" written on the bottom, but was obviously fake even by non-magical creature standards.

The shrill voice of the gnome seemed amplified in the hollow of the tree, but Amry leaned in even further to get a better listen at what the creature was saying. "Frits eh? Shoulda known. Let me have your pass." Ian the gnome teetered as he grabbed the obviously unofficial press pass.

While the gnome looked at the pass, Amry filled with hope that this little trick just might work. The gnome looked at the laminated card and then flung it through an unseen opening into the tree. "Pass denied," he claimed. Amry dove in the direction of the flung pass in hopes that he could get through the opening in the trunk and go with the pass to the Magic Forest.

Instead of catching the pass and getting through the tree, Amry landed on the dirt floor of the tree opening and got a face full of dirt. The cavern filled with shrill laughter which sounded more like a tweeting bird in the beginning of spring mating season.

"I sent that straight to Queen Oletta. No doubt she'll contact your leader for you. No doubt she'll have a little interview of her own. You had better go back to where ya came from you little dust bunny." The gnome placed his hands on his hips and kicked more dirt onto Amry who was barely picking himself off the dirt floor.

Amry finally lifted himself up and shouted, "Who ya calling little, you miniature finger puppet?!" He lifted his leather boot in an effort to threaten to stomp on the gnome.

Onda grabbed Amry by the shoulders. "Don't!" he pleaded, "Gnomes are law enforcement in the Magic Forest. He'll only write you up for aggravated stomping and that'll hurt ElCa's efforts at the council meeting tomorrow."

Amry backed out of the hole, first making sure that no one was watching the skirmish in the hole and no one was.

When he turned back around to view the tree or to send a few choice words to the gnome, he saw Onda scratching his dusty head. "Well, he's gone. I wonder how much damage that little tête-à-tête cost us."

“Let’s just wait here. ElCa should be returning from the AMCS meeting any minute.” Amry rolled his eyes in disgust and stepped away from the center of the tree, just in case ElCa would be arriving in that spot.

Onda wondered, “Should we set up the gear here for the interview or do you have some where else in mind?”

“Here is just perfect.” Amry claimed. As his eyes were focused on a tiny gnome sized sign that read: “NO FRITS ALLOWED” clinging to the wall of the tree trunk.

“Get a good digital image of that sign Onda. We’ll use it as the last visual of the report; and when you are done with that, set up your camera in front of the log out here by the tree entrance. I’ll do the interview from there.”

Onda immediately questioned Amry, “Are ya gonna get all fritriotic again? This is supposed to be a local interest interview not a call for war.”

“Don’t worry Onda,” Amry tried to console his camera man, “I got this under control.”

But he lied. He knew it would be hard to curb his bias towards the inhabitants of the Magic Forest, if that was brought up, of course. So as he watched Onda take the photo of the offensive sign and check the acoustics and lighting; he tried to clear the cobwebs off of his new dust-do, and out of his brain, to make way for ideas about the interview questions.

Just as he was getting settled into his own mind to do some real thinking about how the interview should go, dirt billowed up from the trunk of the tree. It looked like a miniature dust tornado forming all round them.

Onda tapped Amry on the shoulder to get him out of his thoughts and focused on what seemed to be the arrival of the elderly spokesperson for the frit tribe. The leader appeared from the dust wearing a long tan linen robe with a leather belt around his waist. Clinging to the belt was the elder's ornate word feather and two keys. One key, Amry thought, looked like a car key. The other key was larger and had the word "MASTER" written on it. Amry had never noticed the elder wearing that one before and thought that maybe this could be the first line of questioning.

He looked at ElCa's face to get an idea of the mood the leader might be in; and he appeared serious, with the lines of his mouth drawn down, his beard braided formally into seven sections representing the years of a frit's life, and the lines of life and age covering his face seemed to be glowing white hot with passion or maybe anger. Amry wasn't entirely sure so he decided to approach the elder with the caution he might save for walking past a sleeping cat.

The frit leader stepped out of the tree trunk and into the light of the sun and the breeze blowing in the meadow. The white hot glow of the wrinkles on his face seemed to dull as his dusty hair blew in the wind and a smile spread across it.

"Good afternoon Onda, Amry. I thought you might be here." ElCa appeared concerned but quickly gave a grin and placed his arms over the shoulders of both frits and drew them close.

"Let's do this thing," he said with an air of confidence and readiness.

Amry's worry about the interview disappeared. It seemed as if ElCa already knew what Amry had planned and was ready for it. ElCa's demeanor was one of wisdom, council, and hope. Amry's uneasiness towards the offensive sign melted away along with his lingering rage towards the little gnome.

Amry motioned to ElCa to have a seat on the log so Onda could position his camera and check the lighting again. He decided to test the waters a bit and probe their leader for some juicy gossip about the council meeting; but as he opened his mouth to question the elder, he noticed that ElCa was visibly saddened and just staring at the keys on his belt.

He carefully whispered to Onda to turn on the camera but he couldn't seem to get his attention. Onda was obviously preoccupied with something behind him. Amry strained his ears to hear Onda say, "Just shut your dust pan and be as still as a mouse."

Hmm, thought Amry, *maybe he's psyching himself out to be professional during the interview.* He tried to get Onda's attention once again by whistling as loud as he could and motioned, again, to Onda to turn the camera on and start recording.

Onda finally turned around and saw Amry's sign, got things ready, and gave Amry the thumbs up.

"Tonight, I am interviewing one of the Magic Forest's most caring and trusting leaders. He has just returned from the Ancient Magical Creature Society weekly meeting and he's distraught, disappointed, and bemused."

Amry turned to ElCa after this introduction and begin the interviewing process, "Sir, ElCa, can you tell us what is on your mind?"

The wise leader lifted his eyes off of his keys and spoke to the camera, "For years, many years, I have attended council meetings with the leaders of all the Magical creature tribes: the elves, dragons, dwarves, gnomes, fairies, and such. I go every week in the hopes of convincing someone, *anyone*, to take up our cause, to beg Queen Oletta to renew our Ancient Magical Creature Status so that one day we can return to our rightful homes in the Magic Forest, but to no avail."

Amry saw that the wrinkles on ElCa's face were getting whiter and brighter. He immediately thought this might be a good time to interject with some of his feelings about the Queen and her minions.

However, ElCa clearing his throat and continuing his homily stopped him short.

"For years I have pleaded our case, that we have a rich heritage as magical creatures. We coexisted with man from the very beginning of time in some capacity or another. We are recorded in scripture, 'ashes to ashes' being man and 'dust to dust' being the frit. We are recorded in human history as the very dust that covers historical records and family charts in attics, basements, and garages all over the world."

"We even benefit mankind by helping them to forget the silly and corruptible items in their daily lives. In extreme cases I have helped certain humans' progress towards happiness by helping them forget, little by little, their misery and woe of missing a loved one, or losing an object."

"These deeds go unrecorded…unrewarded, as it should be. But in our own history as a people, a member of the Magical Creature Family; we have been forgotten, which is not as it should be. We are erased from the fairytales, the epic trilogies, and the cartoons. We have been denied access to camaraderie and companionship with our kindred spirits, if you will."

"We are not asking for anything hard like justice or mercy. We're just asking for remembrance…for a more secure present and a hope of our future."

ElCa paused and looked at the key on his belt that had the word "MASTER" engraved upon it. Amry thought that maybe now would be a good time to ask a question, but Elca, not wanting his dramatic pause to be interrupted, placed his arm around Amry and continued his speech. "I know that there are some young 3 or 4 year old frits, in the prime of their life, looking for justice, for retaliation by joining a frit organization called the Key-pers. But I plead with you, this is not the way. Seek out your brethren and sistren. Join together in hope, not hate. If the Key-pers continue in their sinister acts of violence towards other creatures of the magic forest realm, it will only serve the purposes of those who despise us."

ElCa stared at Amry with what Amry thought was making him feel a little guilty and uncomfortable. "Act with your heart not your kicking feet or pounding fist. We will be remembered one day. Our status will be renewed one day."

Amry was going to butt in and say his signature sign-off: "Finders Keepers Losers Weepers", but ElCa beat him to the punch.

"I know Amry likes to say, 'Finders Keepers Losers Weepers' at the end of his reports; but I would like to say that the finders of hope and faith who endure are the *winners* and the Key-pers of hate and violence are the *losers* and the cause of the weeping. Carry on my people. Carry on."

Amry wanted to add, "*Truly finders are the winners and Key-pers are a bunch of losers,*" but he thought that ElCa said it better than he ever could. ElCa folded his arms and sat still on the log. Amry signaled to Onda to cut off the camera; but again he noticed that Onda was looking behind him and shooing something away.

"Hey! Onda," Amry tried to get Onda to turn around and face him, "We're done! Cut off the camera!"

Onda refocused his attention on Amry and fiddled with the buttons on the camera to turn it off and start recording the images previously shot.

Amry breathed a sigh of relief. "What a shot of luck!" he exclaimed. "ElCa, you saved me. I had no idea what to ask you, plus you had no intention of answering any questions. Your preaching was just perfect."

"Umm, off-record, can I ask you a question?" The tribal leader nodded in approval so Amry continued, "Did you find out about the gnome, 'cause I'm really sorry about that. I hope he didn't write the whole frit tribe up for 'gnome stomping' or anything like that."

ElCa began to laugh, "Oh, Oh, Oh, my little fritter, you can sure tell that your generation has not been taught much about the Magic Forest and its creatures. That wasn't a gnome, it was a leprechaun. No wonder you got lucky. I was just sitting here wondering why I gave that speech myself. Did the little guy laugh at you?"

Amry searched his memory, "Yeah, yeah he did; albeit a diabolical twirpy kind of laugh."

"Well my son," said ElCa, "leprechaun laughter gives luck to the hearer and besides, you were messing with Ian, the con, leprechaun. He just wanted your ID to get into Magic Forest gatherings and functions."

Amry looked confused, "Well, how do ya know that ElCa?"

The leader replied, "I saw him just before I came through the oak. He was sitting on the forest floor scratching off the name 'Amry' and changing it to 'Ian'. He had also colored in your hair red and your clothes yellow and green. If ya ever wondered what you would look like as a leprechaun? Well, green is your color I think."

Amry and ElCa laughed and climbed off the log. Onda rushed up to meet them with his gear. "Amry, that was fritlicious." Onda exclaimed out of breath.

Amry retorted, "Well I am wondering how much of that interview you actually saw. Every time I tried to get your attention, you were messing with something in the grass behind you." Amry seemed a little perturbed about the whole thing.

Onda squirmed a little before explaining himself, "Oh that?" squirmed Onda, trying to explain himself. "That was just an annoying squirrel." Onda's voice got louder. "HE KEPT TRYING TO EAT MY CHEESE FROM MY SATCHEL SO I TOLD HIM TO GET LOST!!!!!!!!" Onda's voice had gotten really loud. He lowered to normal range and said, "Well, after I yelled at him, I didn't have any more trouble, and here I am."

ElCa leaned over and whispered to Amry, "That's an awfully big squirrel standing over there eating Onda's block of cheese."

Amry looked harder at the tall figure standing in the grass. Onda noticed the figure as well. Both cried in unison: "Yo!"

Onda hurried to explain, "Sorry Amry, he followed us, there was nothing I could do. I know you get flustered when he shows up to your reports, so I just tried to keep it a secret."

"Well, no harm no foul." said Amry as he elbowed his friend.

Yo was now upon the three standing by the log and decided to find his way into the conversation, "You were great Amry. I kept trying to give you the 'thumb's up' sign but Onda kept pushing me back into the grass. Oh and ElCa, it's great to meet you in person. You are inspiring *and* shiny."

The other three frits wondered what Yo meant by that last comment but shrugged it off knowing that he always had a special way of expressing himself.

"Are you heading back to the station boys?" ElCa inquired.

"Yeah, we've got to go over this interview to make it worthy to air in the next…" Amry stopped to look at his large pocket watch, "the next 2 hours. We've gotta get going and I really hope we make it back in time."

ElCa grabbed the Master key from his belt and rubbed it between his thumb and forefinger whispering words only he could hear, Then he said, "Hold hands my little dust bunnies."

Yo asked if they needed to click their heels too, but before ElCa could answer, a whirling gust of wind and dust swirled up over the meadow and scooped them all up. As soon as Amry and the others let out squeals of delight and panic, the frits were dropped down several blocks away at the side yard of the house which held the Fristcovery Channel newsroom in its living room entertainment center.

"Wow, ElCa. What else does that key do?" Amry exclaimed, all the while realizing that a second interview was definitely needed between him and ElCa.

"Oh my son, let not these things trouble you, for one day soon, deeper things will have need of your mindfulness. Save all your fretting for that," ElCa counseled Amry. And with a whoosh of the wind, his dusty hair and beard were swept off of the ground, leaving the three friends amazed and not so much in a hurry to get the report ready.

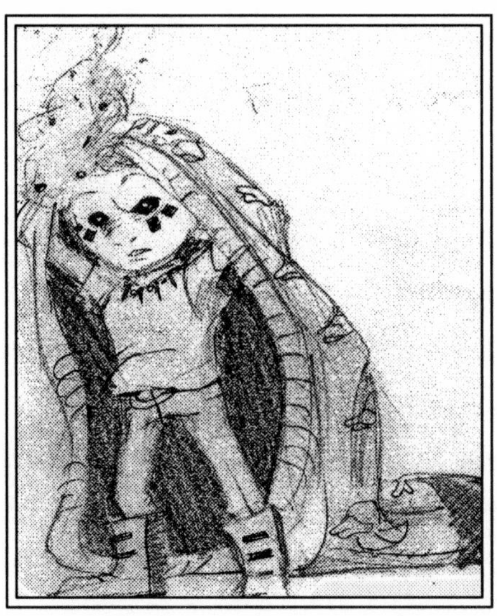

9

Thumb's Up

Standing in the driveway, dusting off the dirt left over from ElCa's way of travel, the three friends jumped because they had all heard it: Junior was in the driveway playing roller hockey. They quickly put their socks on but not before they saw Ishi, the door duty frit, was already beckoning the three pieces of footwear to come inside through the open basement door which he had made Junior forget to shut.

Amry whispered to his friends, "Be *silent* and *play dead*." It was too late to say the forgetting spell this time.

All of the sudden, Junior made a lucky slap shot into the open door of the house. Inside you could hear Mrs. yelling, "JUNIOR, SHUT THE DOOR! How many times do I have to tell you?"

Junior replied, "Mom, I *did* shut the door, the wind must have blown it open." He then muttered to himself, "It is kinda gusty out here anyway.", referring to the swirling dust breeze that just came through.

"Well come on inside," Mrs. said as she gathered her son's sports equipment and paddled him lightly as he came through the doorway. She moved to shut the door when she saw three dirty socks on the edge of the driveway.

"JUNIOR!!!!! I don't remember telling you to put your dirty socks in the driveway. What are you thinking?" She went outside to the driveway and scooped up the socks.

"What do you have in here, rocks? These aren't for rock collections. They are for your feet. Empty them out and put them in the washroom." She handed the socks to her son who, with his roller blades still on, skated over the carpet in the living room to the linoleum in the game room, onto the concrete in the washroom. He systematically, shook the socks out into the garbage bag hanging on the washroom door and threw the socks in the basket next to the washing machine.

For a moment there was silence in the washroom. There was no movement in the garbage bag; and the author of this book was wondering if the story was over.

But after a few minutes, Yo could be heard whimpering, Onda was groaning, and Amry was struggling to clamber out of the trash.

"Oh for dragon's sake!" he said as he gingerly lifted himself over the edge of the garbage bag and dropped to the floor. Reaching up, he pulled the edge of the plastic bag down to see if his friends were still in one piece.

"I think," Onda said, trying to pull himself up out of the garbage and reaching for Amry's out-stretched hand, "I think I liked ElCa's mode of travel better." Amry pulled Onda out and they both began prodding the garbage bag looking for Yo.

"I think we are gonna have to pull this bag down and empty it. Poor Junior, he's probably gonna get in trouble again." Onda began tugging at the black trash bag until it snapped off the handle of the door and fell to the floor. Amry and Onda both saw a long stick figure squirming in the bag and crawling towards the opening. They reached in to help him but were pushed aside by Olet who had seen everything from her job by the washing machine.

"Let me at him." She pushed both frits away from the garbage bag. She called to Yo, "Brother, brother, are you okay? Reach for my hand, dust bunny." Yo moved from the edge of the inside of the bag and let his sister pull him up.

Finally everyone was standing. Yo's balance and sanity had returned to default settings and the three friends decided to make a run for the news channel station, but not before they checked to see if Junior, Mrs., or Mister was around.

However, Olet wasn't quite ready to have them leave yet. "Hey youfers," she yelled. "What have you gotten my brother into?" She was visibly angry and planned to take it out solely on Amry. "Isn't it bad enough you holler at him all day long, but now you have to put him in harm's way?" Olet put her arm around Yo's waist and moved him in the direction of the Wind Star Twin Style Salon.

Amry drew his foot across the floor and made small circles with it. He couldn't even look her in the eye. He knew he hurt her feelings that morning; and he knew that he was constantly making fun of, and excluding, her brother Yo. He really was sorry but it was hard to tell her.

Amry thought, *she is so cute when she is angry. Her cheeks turn pink and her eyes get sparkly.* Amry's romantic thinking was interrupted by a loud thump on his back and a flick on his ear.

"Where did you go just then, Amry? Olet is gone. She took Yo with her. She waited for you to say something, and she left when she saw drool come out your mouth."

Onda giggled as he drew the facts to his friend. "Amry you are a mess, just tell her you like her instead of being mean to her. That doesn't work anymore."

"Obviously," muttered Amry as he picked up his satchel and sock and gestured for Onda to come with him back to the station.

"Should we put these on?" questioned Onda as he held up his red and green argyle sock out of the basket.

"Nah." said Amry, "I think everyone has left the living room and the TV is blaring so loudly that I doubt they would notice two ugly socks sliding across the floor." Amry and Onda headed out of the washroom door to the area behind the love seat. They slid behind the leather piece of furniture and then jumped onto the bottom lip of the entertainment center. They forged back up to the shelves behind the TV to the Fritscovery News Channel Station.

Ocus was waiting for the two man crew at the edge of the VCR. "So how'd it go? I'm sure you worked your friterry air into the dust of the Earth."

Amry and Onda nodded emphatically and stated that they needed to review the report that was now due in exactly an hour. Ocus permitted the two to side step around him and out of the office but not before he called for Amry's attention one more time.

"Um, Amry? Can I count on this interview being nothing less than spectacular?"

Amry silently nodded and ran to catch up with Onda.

"Whew!" said Amry as he wiped his brow.

"Whew, what?" asked Onda.

"Whew, I'm glad the interview went so well that I can get Ocus off my back. Really, at this point, I'm just glad that we're still alive. Let's review this report. I hope I still look good on camera after my hair grew from putting that spell on the gno…oops I mean leprechaun."

"What leprechaun?" Onda seemed confused and wanted clarification.

"I'll tell ya later, let's just edit the report and get it down to broadcasting."

Onda found a place to set down the pen-cam and was going to tell Amry that he was ready to push play, but Amry wasn't around. "Am, where did ya go?" Onda yelled.

Amry yelled back, "I'm going to ask Ishi if he's okay or find out if he got hurt trying to get us back into the house! I'll be right back. You can edit the report without me!"

Onda moved back into position over the camera and pressed "play" to see the recording of Amry's interview with ElCa. He clearly saw the beginning of the report with Amry's introduction of the tribal leader; and then something went wrong with the image.

It went blurry while the leader was giving his speech. Onda let the report run a little more. He noticed that he could clearly see a frit thumb being held upright in front of the camera lens. The thumb was perfectly positioned right over ElCa's face; it never moved until Amry faced the camera to say, "Onda, cut the camera, we're done."

Onda sat there, in front of the camera. His jaw was dropped. His mouth was open to say, “What in the broom just happened?” but he was too bewildered to speak. He heard Amry approachin g and said to himself, “*What are you gonna say to Amry*?” H e stood perfectly still, awaiting inspiration. Amry walked right up to Onda and almost startled him. “Ishi is alright. Mrs. almost stepped on him, but he quickly hid behind the edge of the window seat until she and Junior went back upstairs. How does the report look? Is it ready to go?”

Onda knew, at this point, that telling Amry about the disaster now would only cause more trouble. *Best let the report just run*, he thought *and ask forgiveness later. Okay, here goes nothing.*”

He looked at Amry confidently and said, “It’s great Am. I saw the intro and all, and I’m sure the rest is just fine. I’m gonna send it over to Saab in Broadcasting to get it on the air.”

Amry beamed, “I’m finally glad to have luck on my side. I’ll have to send Ian, the con, leprechaun a thank-you note or maybe a pair of green socks.”

Onda said, “What?”

Amry replied, “Just come back to Ocus’ office when you are done with Broadcasting, we’ll watch the report and then I’ll tell you the whole story.”

Onda’s eyes got wider, and he began to rethink his policy of “asking forgiveness” later; because it might not be offered. Onda walked over to Saab and handed him the memory card from the pen-cam containing the report which may cause the end of his relationship with his best friend.

Saab put the memory card into the slot behind the DVD player and re-hooked some wires into the satellite receiver and sent the report to the Public Access channel.

As he walked down the corridor to Ocus' office, where Amry was waiting, he decided that it might be best if he threw himself back into the garbage bag and save his friend the trouble.

No wait, he suddenly remembered, *I better warn Olet. Amry is going to kill her brother. I told him that Amry did not need a sign of encouragement. I told him to stop holding up his thumb and to stay hidden in the grass, but he never listens. He needs to clean the lint from his ears.* Onda peered over the edge of the VCR shelf to see his boss' office with Amry waiting eagerly inside to see the report come on.

Amry saw Onda and motioned for him to come down and sit next to him to watch the report. "This is gonna be so easy, like hiding in an antique store." Amry said proudly to his friend as he jabbed him in the ribs with his elbow.

Onda thought it was gonna be more like eating glass.

The report started out just as it should have. The shot of Amry and ElCa sitting on the log next to the oak tree was *inspiring*. Amry's introduction of ElCa was *glowing*, and Yo's "thumb's up" sign, perfectly motionless and positioned over ElCa's face during his entire speech was……

"Frenetic!!!!" screamed Ocus. "Do you know what that word means? Huh, do ya?" Amry hung his head once again and kicked Onda with his left boot, hard.

"No sir," he mumbled.

"Frenetic, it's one of those combined words meaning, I'm furious, in a frenzy; I'm going to wring your fritty little neck!" Ocus leaped over the desk and lunged towards Amry with out-stretched arms, when a little birdie chirp could be heard from inside Ocus' jacket pocket. He had fallen into Amry's lap and was finding it hard to reach.

"Can I get that for you, sir?" said Amry as he reached into his boss' pocket to pull out a tiny birdie phone shaped like a hummingbird.

"Very tiny," observed Amry.

"Must be the new prototype," chimed in Onda trying to make small talk and put his feelers out to see if Amry was screaming mad or just disappointed. He found out soon enough.

"Dust off!" yelled Amry and he stood up to lift his boss off of his lap to standing position.

"No, you dust off!" shouted Onda, "It wasn't my fault. There was nothing I could do!"

"Both of you, shut your lint traps!" yelled Ocus, "I'm on the birdie phone here." Ocus opened the hummingbird so that its wings stuck straight out and put his ear right next to the birdie's beak. Amry and Onda listened closely, eavesdropping for any sign of redemption or complaint.

"Who am I speaking to? Yes, okay, well that's not the way I saw it but, okay."

Amry and Onda knew this must be a viewer calling with criticism. They tried to leave the office but Ocus, with one hand, grabbed Amry and pulled him back in and grabbed Onda and pulled him back in as well.

He then resumed his conversation. "Yes, well, I highly doubt I have enough trust left for him to do that." Ocus shot a pointing glance at Amry while continuing his phone conversation. "Well, it would be a great story. You say this is the way you want it done and Amry is the one you want doing it? Is your dust on right? Okay then, I'll have him get back to you. Oh, *you* want to contact him? Oh I see, Okay. Call the station when you are ready. Thank you. No, no. no. Thank you." Ocus closed his birdie phone; put it back in his jacket pocket, and pushed Amry and Onda back into their chairs.

"Seems as though your little stunt today with ElCa's face being covered during his entire speech, is exactly what someone wants you to do again when interviewing them. Could this have to do with the luck you received from encountering a leprechaun's laugh today?" Ocus teased Amry.

Amry simply shrugged his shoulders.

Ocus continued, "Well, let's just say that leprechaun luck only lasts for so long before it turns into downright misery. Did ElCa give you that little bit of information?"

Amry shrugged again, and said to Onda, "Ian can forget me sending him green socks then. I have half a mind to send him an angry cockroach."

Ocus grabbed Amry by the chin to get his full attention. "However, seeing as you just received your first request to be an investigative reporter; I would say that your luck is holding on by a tiny speck of dust." Ocus finished the ribbing of his employee and began writing on a yellow sticky pad with a tiny ink pen refill.

Amry was afraid to ask what the investigation entailed. *Better not kick a gift horse in the mouth,* he thought. "Okay, Ocus, tell me what to do to redeem myself. I'll do anything."

Then Amry turned to Onda and finished his request, "but, I'll need my own camera that I can work with a remote. I'm not using Onda this time around. I'll film myself."

Onda twiddled his fingers knowing that he expected nothing less. He had let Amry down. He was asked to not bring Yo to the interview. However, he couldn't help the fact that Yo just showed up on his own accord. Surely Amry could forgive him that.

Onda excused himself from the office. He decided to head over to the Wind Star Style Salon and check on Yo, and maybe look for a new job as a hair model photographer.

As he left, he could hear Ocus telling Amry the specifics of the job, something about the Key-pers, something about witness protection, something about…oh forget it. Onda waved his hand at the office and walked down the long corridor behind the entertainment center to head out to the washroom. Yo would always be there for him.

10

The Key-pers

"Amry get over here and watch the rest of the news. This is what your investigative report is to entail," Ocus pointed to the small playback screen on the digital camera that was hooked up to the satellite receiver. Amry followed his boss' orders and watched Rove, the Fritscovery news anchor, giving a special breaking news report.

"Rove here for a Fritscovery News channel breaking story. Earlier this afternoon, another frit was threatened with the resurfacing of his birth keys in front of their owners. This would surely spell death as we all know.

The frit, who at this time, must remain anonymous, was approached by the Key-pers, the frit organization bent on performing acts of mischief and violence towards all other magical creatures until our status is renewed.

He was told that, if he did not join the Key-pers and help them with their dastardly deeds, his birth-keys would "magically" be found by their owner in the ignition of their birth car, and then the frit would die. He immediately took his story to the authorities in the hopes that his life may be spared.

The authorities have asked this frit's father where his birth-keys were hidden, but the father apparently was visited by the Key-pers as well, to learn the keys' location, and he is too shaken to talk.

When will this end? We have been asked by our leader ElCa to stop these acts of violence for they only hurt our cause with the Fairy Queen and her council. If you can avoid joining the Key-pers, do so. If you are threatened by members of their organization, come to the authorities at once. You don't have to join. We will do all we can to help you. We can resolve our status renewal without violence. This is Rove for the Fritscovery News Channel news signing off."

Amry eyes opened wide, *oh cheese,* he thought, *Elca must really hate me. He is throwing me right into harm's way. Guess I deserve that. Even greater. Seems like I need Onda to work the camera and I need Yo's thumb; and he won't come unless Onda is coming. Great.* He turned to his boss and asked for the details of the interviewee who requested his services.

"All I can tell you, Amry, is that he is a defector. He apparently was approached, by the Key-pers and apparently he joined. He wants to defect, but they won't let him. They are threatening him with his birth-keys being found as well."

"It seems as though the Key-pers are running low on volunteers to go to the Magic Forest and wreak havoc on the queen's dominion, so now they have to resort to death threats to get new members. No wonder, either, if you can actually get into the Forest, the gnomes are everywhere and they report you as soon as you step foot through the oak and the queen's rage is nothing short of electrifying, from what I hear. This frit is supposed to contact you when he is ready for you to interview him." Ocus pulled out the sticky pad he had written on earlier while he was conversing with the Key-per.

"Well is there anything else you can give me to go on? I would like to prepare for this report. I don't really know much about their organization, except that I have tried to stay clear of it for a while now, and now I am going to be thrown smack down into the dust." Amry started to pace around the office chewing on his bottom lip.

Ocus peered down at the yellow paper on his desk and spoke softly, "Okay, listen Amry, since I am at the top of a newsroom, well, I hear things. The only thing I know is that the leader of the Key-pers is a no nonsense frit they call 'Vipe'. He claims to know where his birth keys are. Consequently, they will never be found, and he can never die."

"He uses this knowledge to gain the respect of frits who have an inclination towards usurping power and committing acts of violence and hate. That's all I know, but don't put it out there that I told you. They could come after me, and if I go, you go!" Ocus held up his hands in disgust. "Why don't you go and ask ElCa what he knows? You seemed to be buddy buddy with him during your interview."

Amry piped up, "Umm Ocus, why did this frit want me to do the interview in the first place?"

"Oh that," remembered Amry's boss, "he thought it clever that you covered ElCa's face with Yo's thumb. He thought you were trying to protect his identity in case any rogue magical creatures were watching and wanted to get a good look at the leader to find him in a crowd and take him out. It seems like he wants you to use the same type of technique to keep his identity secret."

"Guess Yo's mistake wasn't too bad of a thing. Oh, and about that, you're going to need Yo, which means you're going to need Onda. I don't see him in here. What did you do?"

Amry frowned, he had kicked Onda pretty hard, not to mention he had told him to "dust off". Amry thought for a second and then replied to his boss, "Don't worry, I'll get Onda and Yo back."

"Well, you better, 'cause this might be the greatest report of your career." Ocus grinned and added, "or, at least the most death defying. Just think. I could have you out of my hair forever."

"Ocus!!!?" screamed Amry. "Why would you say something like that?" Then Amry muttered under his breath, *"'Cause you don't have much hair for me to be into."*

Ocus pushed Amry out of his office and added, "I heard that. Don't you have an interview to do, instead of getting cheeky with me? The frit said he would call your birdie phone when he was ready with a secure location to meet. Go wait somewhere else instead of getting dust all over my office."

This statement had just reminded Amry that he had a lavender lint wig in his satchel to give to his boss, as a joke. Ocus was balding quite a bit and was very sensitive about it. Amry pushed his new found luck one more time as he pulled the wig out of his satchel. "Oh boss, I got you something for your dust issue, Wind and Star say it's the next big thing in frit fashion, hope it fits that big head of yours," and with that, Amry ran out of Ocus' office, and headed out to make amends with Onda, and to threaten Yo within an inch of his life if he didn't do exactly what he was told.

Hmm, where to look, thought Amry as he headed down the corridor behind the VCR, and back to his office. Amry noticed that there was a note on his desk.

Am,

I am sorry that I let you down. I am leaving my camera with you to use for your investigative report. I have attached to this note a

set of instructions on how to run the camera and all. If you need my help, I will be at the Wind Star Style Salon.

Amry looked at the attached set of instructions, and realized that Onda's handwriting left a lot to be desired. Not to mention the schematics for all the buttons and dials were too much for Amry's brain to handle in a stressful situation like this.

"*Okay, I'll go to the salon. But that means seeing Olet, and it means pretending not to be mad at Yo again!*" Amry realized that he was talking to himself out loud as another news anchor passed by and asked Amry if he needed some frit counseling to help him with his mental issues. He shrugged, put on his satchel around his chest, and loaded up his sock, birdie phone, and Onda's camera.

UMMF, this weighs a ton. No wonder Onda always packs food to eat. I wouldn't be able to keep my strength up for nothing trying to carry all of this if I wasn't snacking twenty-four-seven.

He headed out of the office and through the left side entrance to venture back into the washroom, right at the sight where his luck had started to run out. *Didn't ElCa say something about saving all my worrying for some misery that was coming my way? I wish our leader would give a time line when he gives advice.* Amry came to a stop by the entertainment center just in time to see Mister, the father of the house, smack in front of the TV, eating and watching the news.

Cheese, how am I gonna get past him this time. Amry surveyed the living room, to figure out just what he could make Mister forget so that he could get by.

Okay let's see what we have here. We've got a blanket that's not been folded up, several DVDs laying on the floor, some cookie crumbs and… TADA.!! Amry found the perfect item for Mister to forget. He hated getting the man in trouble, but why stop being consistent now.

Amry pulled out his feather and began his charm, "May your forgetfulness be dust upon the heads of all frits present, forget that you are sitting next to a large glass of root beer. May your forgetfulness be dust upon the heads of all frits present."

Amry waited to see if his plan had worked. He watched Mister as he fiddled with the remote, and became animated with the rising tension of the anchorman's voice. Amry's bangs began to grow right as Mister flicked off the TV and reached for his newspaper. The cup of root beer sitting right next to him on the end table spilled all over the light colored carpet. Some of the root beer began to seep into the legs of Mister's pants.

"Aww man, the wife is *not* going to like this, and I was being careful." Mister exclaimed as he bounded up the stairs to get a wet washcloth and some carpet cleaner out from under the kitchen sink.

Amry knew that it was time to bolt. *No need to put the sock on now, get moving,* he encouraged himself and steadily climbed down off of the entertainment center and carefully moved quickly across the game room linoleum and to the washroom door that was not open.

Dust bunnies, thought Amry, *How am I going to get in?* Amry waited a few moments and heard Mister leaping down a few stairs at a time. *Wait, wait,* he told himself. *Mister is going to have to put that dirty washcloth somewhere. Let's hope he remembers to put it in the washroom. Side bar. I wish that as a frit I also had a remembrance charm, that would also come in handy.* .Amry pulled his pink sock with white ducks out of his satchel and put it on. He waited by the washroom door behind the vacuum cleaner.

Mister sprayed the carpet, blotted the offending stain away, and headed straight for the washroom. At exactly this moment, right when Amry was ready to come out from the vacuum and follow Mister into the washroom, Amry's satchel began to chirp.

Mister opened the washroom door and Amry jumped through the door and hid by the laundry detergent on the floor next to the garage door. Amry's birdie phone was really chirping now, and Mister had heard it.

"Honey, I think that a bird got into the house, and is down here in the washroom!" Mister yelled upstairs to his wife and awaited her reply.

He searched for the broom in the washroom to sweep the bird out of its hiding place. Amry chose this moment to make a break for the Wind Star Salon behind the dryer. As he passed through the dryer sheet, he reached into his satchel and opened the phone.

Amry whispered into the phone, "Don't hang up. I am in a tight spot right now, just be as quiet as you can be." Amry put the phone down by his feet and gestured to the surprised customers in the salon to be quiet because Mister was following the sound of the birdie phone. Silence fell over the hair salon as the frits could hear the sweeping of a broom.

"Here birdie, birdie, birdie," said Mister as he looked and listened for the bird in the house. Mister's broom was coming straight for the space between the washer and the dryer. Amry and the salon patrons scooted up against the back wall.

Mister moved the broom back and forth like a hockey stick until it clanged with an object on the floor: Amry's phone. Mister used the broom to slide the phone out from behind the two appliances.

"Oh for the queen's sake!" whispered Wind. Amry shook his hand at the twin in an effort to silence her. He watched in horror as his phone was swept away by Mister.

"A baby toy? Hmm. It must have been left here when Junior was little," said Mister as he looked at it on the floor right at the edge of the washing machine.

Amry thought that if he could just muster up enough courage he could pick up the birdie phone and make a run for it.

He started to make his way down the aisle by the dryer and Onda pulled him back, "Just let it go," he whispered into Amry's ear, dragging him away from the edge of the phone and Mister's broom.

Mister finally pulled the toy all the way out and carried it over to the garbage that he noticed was spilled out all over the floor.

"I guess I should throw this toy away and get this trash off the floor and outside, since it is trash day tomorrow."

Amry, Onda, Yo, Olet, and all the others were watching from behind the utility sink as Mister picked up all the garbage, along with the phone, tied up the garbage bag, and carried it through the washroom door and out to the garage door which he lifted up with the garage door opener in his pocket.

The frits walked back into hiding behind the dryer, and they could hear Mister throwing the bag into a garbage can and rolling it all the way down to the bottom of the driveway. They heard Mister close the garage door with the remote and re-enter the house through the front door.

Everyone moved back inside the salon. Amry noticed as he sat down on an empty box of dryer sheets that everyone was staring at him.

Wind approached him first, "Honey, do you have an accident gnome following you around? I didn't see one; but he could be hiding very well."

"No, I'm just working off the misery left over from some leprechaun luck that I stepped in this afternoon." Amry put his hands over his eyes as Onda sat down on the box next to him.

"Who was on the little birdie?"

"I think it was my career calling me to say that it was going down the toilet and wouldn't be coming back up."

"No really," said Onda, "who was it?"

"Well, I think it was the guy that I was supposed to interview while he is incognito."

Yo came over to his friends and interjected, "Cheetos? I love cheetos."

"No ya dumb twit, incognito. It means in disguise or unrecognizable. Anyway, Ocus said that he was an ex- Key-per."

At the moment that Amry said "Key-per", two new frits appeared at the front of the salon. "Did someone call for me?" Amry recognized the voice at once and turned to see his friend Tang in the doorway. Tang turned from the frit that he had come in with and walked over to Amry.

"Did someone say Key-per?" Tang smiled mischievously, and stretched out his hand to pat Amry on the back. Amry moved off of the box he was sitting on to avoid contact with his wayward friend.

"Look Tang, I told you how I feel about you joining that group of miscreants. Don't act like we're still going to hang out, 'cause we're not. I won't do the things that you're into now. You're on the wrong side of the fight Tang." Amry tried to walk further away from his friend, but Tang pulled him back.

Tang looked around the salon to see if the companion he walked in with was paying any attention to him, and then he leaned in to whisper to Amry. Tang's mood was serious, "You're right Amry, I am on the wrong side of the ff……." Tang stopped cold.

The frit who had walked in with him was approaching him with a look of disapproval. Tang continued, "..the wrong side of the fight. If you call the wrong side the winning side. I saw your little report about ElCa, what little I could see through Yo's thumb, and believe me, youfers are the losers." And with that Tang pointed to everyone in the salon.

Amry told his friend to cut it out and just leave.

Tang's companion took him by the arm, took something out of his pocket, and handed it to him. Tang reluctantly held out what looked like Amry's birdie phone, for everyone to see.

Tang's companion began to speak, "Seems like on our way here, we performed a service for you. But seeing as our kind isn't wanted here, maybe our services aren't either."

Tang immediately pulled the phone out of Amry's grasp as he reached for it and then teased him by holding it out and offering it again. This time, Amry was quick enough to snatch it back and started looking it over for garbage or scratches.

"How did you get this?" Amry questioned his friend.

"Mister was still pondering over it in the driveway, and we simply made him forget about it. His loss is our gain right? Finders keepers, losers weepers, right Amry?"

"Thank you but you had better leave now. I appreciate you getting back my phone." And just as Amry said the word "phone", his phone rang, to which Tang bellowed, "Is there a birdie in the house Mister?"

He and his companion left the salon, and Amry answered his phone. "Yes? Oh yes, I'm sorry about that. Where do you want to meet? Sure we'll be there in 20 minutes." Amry closed his phone and looked it over. He still couldn't believe he had destroyed and revived his career in 1 day. He headed back over to the dryer sheet box where Yo and Onda were talking.

On his way, he was pushed over by Star who was pushing salon customers over to get to Amry quickly. "I wouldn't touch that phone if I were you. Who knows what they've done to it."

"It's okay," said Amry, "Tang may have joined the Key-pers, but he wouldn't let anything bad happen to me."

Star rebutted, "I wouldn't be so sure. Maybe he doesn't have a choice. Just be careful." And she walked back over to her station and began talking furiously with Wind and Olet.

"Frit ladies." Amry shook his head and mumbled as he got back over to Onda and Yo.

"Listen youfers, I was wrong to dismiss you so easily this evening. You know I could never do a report without you, Onda. Come on, I can barely carry this thing." Amry took the camera out of his satchel and struggled to give it to his cameraman.

Amry continued, "And Yo, well, I actually need your help this time. See, your thumb in the way is exactly what this frit needs to be interviewed incognito, not cheeto."

"Oh," said Yo as he dug the heel of his shoe into the ground.

"Look, I know this is going to be dangerous, so I am going to say this up front. This interview is going to require a little more frit finesse and focus than the last one. So let's all be on the same page here."

Onda and Yo nodded their heads in agreement.

"Okay, Amry but where are we going, who are we interviewing, and why does Yo's thumb need to be in the way?"

Yo nodded, "Yeah Am, do I really get to come to this report? You mean I don't have to hide or pretend to show up late?"

"No, Yo. You can come. Your thumb is requested and required."

"What for?" asked Yo. "Do I get to paint a face on it and let *it* do the interview?"

Amry and Onda chuckled; truly, Yo was an idiot, no doubt.

"Just come on, let's get all our gear together and I'll tell you on the way."

Amry and Onda began to pack up Onda's camera gear into his sling, and Yo walked over to Olet's work station to talk to his sister.

Amry was about to motion to Yo that it was time to go when Olet left her work station in a hurry, and ran over to Amry. "Nuh-uh. Not this time. You are *not* taking Yo with you. I am *not* pulling him out of another garbage can, and I am *not* letting you yell at him anymore for things he does that he just can't control." Olet turned to see Yo at her station trying on wig after wig.

"Yo tells me that you're taking him to do an interview that involves disguising Cheetos or something like that. Well I won't have it. He's not a toy Amry. You just can't carry him with you and take him out and play with him any time you want." Olet was wringing her hands and stomping as she talked.

Amry decided to follow Onda's advice from this afternoon and say something nice. "Olet, I will watch over Yo. He is my friend. He's also the brother of someone who I care about very much, even if I don't act like it." Amry lowered his head so that he was eye to eye with Olet.

She wouldn't look at him, but she did say something to him, "Fine, just bring him back in one piece and not in trouble. He looks up to you, ya know."

"I know, and I'll take care of him, don't worry." Amry gave a wink to Olet who had lifted her head to see Amry, and she winked back.

"Yo, Amry, let's go!" yelled Onda from the dryer sheet door of the salon. He had his camera gear packed up in his sling and was ready to go. Yo got out of Olet's chair, grabbed a couple of wigs and his sock, and shoved them in the bag he was wearing across his shoulder and met Amry on the way who had gathered his sock and phone and placed them in his satchel across his chest.

The three friends headed out of the salon behind the washer and the dryer. Onda, who had walked ahead stopped at the intersection of the washroom door to the living room and the washroom door to the garage, "So which way Am?" Onda pointed with both his hands to the door on the left and then the door on the right.

Amry looked through the cracked opening of the washroom door to the garage and noted that the garage door was shut by Mister. "Guess, the only way to go is through the basement door, or up the stairs and out the back door by the kitchen."

"Well, where are we going?" asked Yo who was busy fiddling with the wig he had borrowed from the salon, trying to get it on his head.

Amry snatched the wig from Yo, and put it in his satchel. "We're going to the auto graveyard in Mr. Paul's back yard. You know how he has been collecting old cars and car parts. The frit who wants to be interviewed in private decided that the graveyard would be a good place to go, because it's dark, and has lots of crevices to hide in so that no one sees us."

"Oh yeah, in cogcheeto, right Am?", Yo added, pulling yet another wig out of his satchel and trying that one on.

"Right Yo," Amry was being sarcastic; but this was a battle he was not going to win so, he let it go.

Onda lifted up his sling with all the camera gear and prepared to go but not before he was sure that Amry knew what they were getting in to.

"Amry, is this dangerous? Should we be protecting ourselves or using back-up or something like that?"

Amry thought for a moment and realized out loud, "Youfers are all the protection and back-up that I need. I'm glad that you're with me." Amry, Onda, and Yo once again, friends, headed through the living room, which was dark because the family had gone to bed. They waved to Niss guarding the very small crack of the opened front door. Amry's luck was still holding on.

11

Fritness Protection Program

The three friends, without their socks, without trepidation, and most would say after the fact, without their brains, headed through Farmer Clark's side yard. They worked their way through the backyard of non-growing popsicle sticks, over Mr. Paul's side yard and through the chain link fence of his backyard. They all stood in amazement at the complexity of the pathway through the old automobiles and the car parts strewn through the yard like a giant maze.

Even though it seemed as if everything was located haphazardly, there did seem to be a reason to the madness. Mr. Paul always had his own way of organizing things for his hobby of fixing cars and motorcycles, much to the chagrin of Mrs. Paul who thought of it more as a nuisance than a leisure activity.

"What do we do now? I mean, where are we supposed to meet this joker? Are we just supposed to guess what car part or car he is hiding under? We could be here all night," Onda said wearily as he set down his heavy camera gear.

Amry ventured out from the opening in the fence and began walking down a path, barely visible, that seemed to lead straight from the chain link fence to an old aqua leather bench seat that Amry thought must have belonged to one of those old classic cars that he had seen in Mr. Paul's garage a time or two.

It was dark and Amry didn't realize that he could barely see his hand in front of his face until his birdie phone started ringing.

Onda and Yo came running up to Amry. "Answer it, answer it," said Onda impatiently. I bet it's him. He'll tell us where to meet him."

Amry felt in his satchel for the outline of a bird and pulled out his phone that was now chirping what seemed like louder than before. Amry was puzzled, "I didn't know you could alter the volume on the birdie phone, I always thought they came preset. I must have done it accidentally."

Onda whispered, "It's probably because everything is so quiet out here in the dark. Answer your phone before the owner of this junkyard decides to hunt cardinal for breakfast in the morning."

"Don't be silly Onda, Mr. Paul doesn't eat cardinal; though I am pretty sure he eats turkey. Furthermore, even if I did have a turkey phone, they wouldn't make a birdie phone that big, would they?"

Onda retorted, "I heard your mom had one that big, now answer the phone before I put that bird out of its misery."

Amry picked up his phone and heard the caller say, "I can see you now. I am behind the aqua car seat. Who are the other frits with you? I only asked for you."

Amry closed his phone and whispered into the night air, "This is my camera man Onda and this is Yo, the owner of the thumb which will be used to disguise your identity. Show yourself."

A heavy set frit, wearing an old sweater and his dust slicked back, appeared from behind the bench seat. "I guess they'll be okay. They won't tell anyone they saw me, will they?"

Amry approached the frit and shook his large hand. "No, your identity is safe with all of us. Now, I never caught your name, do you even want to give it to me?"

The husky frit pulled on a thread sticking out from the bottom of his sweater and commenced in tugging on the long strand before he spoke again, this time much more softly than before, "My name is Odge, I trust that you won't use it in the interview, right?"

"Like I said, we've got you covered. We're going to put your story out there so that other frits will know what you've gone through. Maybe this will save a life that I am worried about."

Amry started to take his microphone out of his bag and unwrapped the wire. He took the wire over to Onda to plug into the pen-cam and worked with Onda to make sure that the camera had its flash on for lighting.

Amry went back over to the aqua bench seat and told Odge to sit to the right so that Amry could sit on his left. "Yo is going to position his thumb right over the camera lens so that your face is covered. I will not ask you your name. I will not reveal who you are. However, I *will* let the frit world know that you belong to the Key-pers, and you have been desperately trying to leave all of that. Are you ready?"

Odge sat with his one hand in his lap, and the other hand pulling out more of the string on his sweater. "Uh yeah, I'm ready. Are you sure this is going to work?"

Amry leaned over to look into Odge's eyes to see if he could emotionally make it through the interview and could see some courage there.

"Look, I will check with Yo one more time and look through the lens to make sure that you are completely covered by his thumb. I'll be right back."

Amry ran over to Onda and Yo. He checked the image of Odge as Yo held up his thumb and gave a serious speech to Yo about what to do if his arm got tired. He instructed Onda to look through the lens at all times to make sure that everything was as it should be.

Both his friends let him know that they were 100 percent ready to go. Amry said "good luck" to his crew and headed back to the seat.

Onda whispered, "On one, two, and three…"

"Amry here, for a Fritscovery News Channel exclusive, an interview from a Key-per, who is being held in the organization against his will. For now, we will call him 'Auto' for anonymity."

"So Auto, can you tell us a little about the organization that you are so desperately trying to leave?" Amry held out the microphone to Odge.

"Yes, Amry, the Key-pers are a group of frits who strongly believe that our status as an Ancient Magical Creature cannot be renewed without the use of violence and the misuse of our magic forgetfulness. They believe that it is necessary to 'persuade' members of the AMCS council with small acts of aggression and nuisance in order to get the votes in the renewal process, which I might add is coming up in a few days."

Odge made sure that his head and body remained stiff as he talked so that his profile was held under Yo's thumb in the view of the camera.

"Can you tell us examples of these acts so that we can understand what the Key-pers might ask its members to do?" Amry gave a smile to let Odge know that the interview was going well.

"Well, as a new member of the Key-pers, you are drilled on the long history of the war of nuisance. Ancestors of the Key-pers were not thrilled with all of the new magical creatures moving in and gaining status. They used their magic to cause trouble with some of the other creatures of the forest. They made Cinderella lose her slipper. This caused the Fairy Queen's mother (Fairy Godmother) great distress in getting that story back together. Another pre-exile Key-per thought it would be fun to make some weird looking creature to forget where he hid a ring of power, which put the elves in great distress when another odd looking creature found it. That was, I guess, a deed that they are profoundly proud of. Another deed I am familiar with is when Master Dragon Ragule's brother's egg was found by a human instead of a dragon rider. Master's mother had to go on an arson spree just to get the egg back into the Magic Forest. Imagine how many frits would have to combine their forgetting powers to make humans forget they saw a dragon. I know for a fact there is no sock big enough to cover that problem." Odge giggled a little but quickly returned to his serious mood.

"Auto, how do the Key-pers get into the Magic Forest to play their tricks on the other Ancient Magical Creatures, because it is widely known that frits do not have the password to get in?'

"This, I do not know, Amry. I have only been a member of the Key-pers for a week or two. I guess, information like that is only held by their leader." Odge began to fiddle with his sweater string again.

"Auto, can you tell us the name of the Key-per leader?" Amry already knew the name that his boss had given him earlier, but felt it necessary to hear it from someone on the inside.

"Um, yes, his name is Lord Vipe." Odge stopped pulling on his sweater string and straightened his posture again to avoid moving away from Yo's thumb still being held up over the camera lens.

"Auto, if I may, can I ask you why being a Key-per is so dangerous and what has made you want to disassociate yourself from their organization?" Amry gave Odge the number one sign just to let him know that this was the last question.

"Amry, the Key-pers' name refers to the fact that they hold keys that don't belong to them. They get into the Magic Forest and threaten magical creatures with forgetting charms and aggression. When the queen finds out, she sends out her electric charges from her scepter and for the frit, that means death. Electricity and dust do not mix, so basically, you fry. Most frits who join the organization and do their first deed in the Magic Forest, see this and want to leave. This holding of keys is where the danger lies for one who wants to leave the organization."

"As we all know, frits usually live about 7 years. This is because when a frit is born, the father hides the keys to the car that the frit was born in. The owner of the car usually gets a new set made. However, the car owner usually finds the original keys within 7 years; and when this remembrance happens, the frit whose keys were found turns into a single strand of dust. This is the normal life span of a frit. However, if you join the Key-pers and you want to leave, they....they..."

Odge was hesitating, and Amry grabbed his arm gently to let him know that he was there for him. So, Odge continued, "They go to your father. They threaten him until he gives up the location of your keys. They take your keys and place them back in the ignition of the car in which you were born. If you don't reach them in time, the car owner finds them and then you are dust to dust, my friend, dust to dust, gone before it's your time."

"Vipe, the leader claims that he found out where his keys were (from his father) and stole them so that they would never be found, so that he can live forever. Normal frits don't do that. It's not the way. We are not meant to be immortal; our dust can't handle the years. Anyway, I am sure now that my keys are in the ignition of the car that I was born in. That's why I am doing this interview, so that others can know of the dangers of becoming a Key-per. They can learn from my mistake before I become a single strand of dust to be swept away and thrown out with the garbage."

Odge gave Amry the "cut the camera" sign and Amry signed out with "Finders? Key-pers? Losers? Weepers? What does it all mean? You decide. This is Amry for the Fritscovery news channel."

Amry then whispered to Yo and Onda to push the "stop" button on the camera. He hopped down and asked Odge to follow him behind the aqua bench seat.

"Odge, I am truly sorry for what has happened to you. I admire your courage for coming forward. Is there anything that I can do?"

Amry watched as Odge started to roll the long strand of yarn off his sweater into a ball. "Can you see if my dad still knows where my keys are, or if Vipe has already gotten them? I can't go myself."

"Why can't you go to your dad? I am sure he's worried sick about you?" Amry tried to rub Odge's shoulders to help him get back his courage.

"No, my father thinks I am dead. I joined the Key-pers because I thought it would help me be stronger. All it did was turn me into an even bigger coward. My dad said that I was dead to him if I joined. I haven't spoken to him since."

"You're not a coward." Amry tried to comfort Odge.

"Yes, I am," replied Odge. "I even went to the authorities and they put me in the Fritness Protection Program so that I'd get a new identity. It's kind of fritless really, seeing as soon as the Key-pers get my birth keys, I am dust on the bottom of their shoes."

"Aww Odge, don't think like that. Look, here's what I'll do. If you give me your father's name and address, I will go to him, ask if he still knows where the keys are, and if the key-pers have approached him yet."

Odge and Amry were exchanging information about the Fritness Protection Program, and about Odge's dad's whereabouts, when Onda and Yo showed up with all the gear packed up and ready to go.

Onda handed Amry his microphone rolled up and said, "Odge, that was great, truly you are a hero for just *telling* your story."

Then he turned to Amry and said, "However, we gotta get going, I am sure that Ocus is going to want this report ready to preview by tomorrow morning to make sure that we didn't commit any serious blunders."

Amry nodded his head yes and turned back to Odge, "Can I call you when I get to your father's house?"

Odge shook his head no and told Amry that he would call him tomorrow night around 10 p.m., that was part of the rules of the Fritness Protection Program. All the frits said their goodbyes to Odge as he disappeared behind the aqua leather car seat.

Walking back through the chain link fence and across Farmer Clark's back yard to the front door where Niss was now on duty, Amry asked his friends if they would be willing to help out with Odge's request.

All agreed that they would help for the greater fritty good. Yo and Onda headed back to the TV station to watch the report to make sure it was just right this time.

Amry crawled into the shoe closet and fell asleep, thinking, *I am sure glad my luck held out till tonight. Seems like the misery that ElCa mentioned is on its way. Better get a good night's sleep. Tomorrow the frit world will be mortified and mucky with the showing of this report.*

12

If you give a frit a key, then he'll ask for a....

Ocus stared at his employees, Onda, Amry, and Yo. He had his pointer finger on the memory card of the interview Amry had done with Odge from the night before. Amry crossed his fingers as tightly as he could hoping that this was not going to be another fritastic disaster.

Ocus calmed his fears, "I've seen the report and it is good. It seems as though you three are working great as a team and finally producing quality work. I'll be delighted to run it tonight." Ocus shook the frits hands and congratulated them on a job well done.

"Furthermore, ElCa apparently wasn't too disappointed with his own speech. He thought that Yo's thumb over his face made the whole report interesting to watch; and he thinks you rose to the occasion and is offering you a once in a lifetime opportunity, *all of you.*"

Onda piped up, "What? Do we get to be his brute squad and beat up some Key-pers?"

"No, actually he is going to the AMCS council meeting at the queen's castle in the Magic Forest; and he wants you guys to represent the frit press. Do you know which meeting this is?"

"Is this the one where they vote?" asked Amry.

"No, this is the meeting where each magical creature tribe leader gives their preliminary vote and the reasons behind it; it's like a pre-voting vote meeting," said Ocus as he raised his eyebrows knowing that that did not sound right, but it was right just the same.

"So when is this going to take place?" inquired Amry.

"Well, I believe ElCa said the meeting starts at 11:00 a.m. human time; but that you are to meet him at the Great Oak at 10 a.m. with Onda and Yo and all your gear. He'll bring you up to speed on the rules of being in the press at the council meeting and all of that."

Amry gathered Onda and Yo into his little cubicle. "Look youfers, we need to know how to approach our schedule for today. Odge's father's house is three blocks from here."

Onda interrupted, "Yes, but three blocks is an awfully long distance for our little legs to travel. How are we going to get to his father's house and back to the playground oak tree by 10 a.m.? Its 8 a.m. right now; we only have two hours. It would take us that long just to walk three blocks. I don't think we're going to be able to do this." Onda walked around Amry's desk and sat down on the floor checking to make sure that his battery was charged for the day.

"ElCa's key would come in real handy about now," said Amry as he sat at his desk wondering how they were going to complete their tasks on time or at all.

"Well what I like to do is go to school." Yo had sat down on Amry's desk and was drawing doodles on a small scrap of paper.

"What are you talking about Yo?"

"I like going to school," Yo repeated his statement and jumped off the desk. "Come on youfers, let's go."

Yo motioned to Onda to pick up his gear and head out the door. Amry, who was curious at Yo's statements followed. They each put on their socks and started to exit the entertainment center.

"Look, Yo. You're going to have to be a little more specific. You can't just throw it out there that you like going to school. What school? Flight school? School of Cosmetology? Frit School? We were all home schooled and we're done with that now." Amry silently questioned why he and Onda were following Yo out to the foyer.

Yo said as they passed through the open living rooms doors into the foyer, "I like going to Junior's school."

"What?' said Onda and Amry. Both their interests were now peaked.

"I'm learned," said Yo as he picked up Amry and placed him on his shoulders.

"Whoa, slow down there frit olay. What am I looking for here on your shoulders?"

Yo continued, "Look up there on the window seat. Junior leaves his backpack there and sometimes I get in it and ride the big yellow bus to school. I don't even have to wear my sock either. If Junior sees me in his backpack, he thinks I am a toy. I just do what you tell me to do all the time, 'Be dead and play quietly'."

Amry got off of Yo's shoulders and onto the window seat to take a look at the backpack.

Onda asked Yo to pick him up and carry him to the window seat as well. “So, Yo, what does this have to do with getting to Odge’s father’s house three blocks from here?”

Yo lifted Onda up to the backpack and then pulled himself up. “Junior is almost done with breakfast. When he comes down those stairs, he picks up the backpack with us in it; and we can ride the bus. We’ll travel three blocks in no time at all. Oh Oh, be quiet and play dead. I hear Junior coming.”

All three frits climbed in the open pocket of Junior’s book bag and followed Yo’s advice. Junior leaned over to place some papers and sharpened pencils in his backpack when Yo said as quickly as he could, “May your dust be forgetfulness on the heads of all frits present. Don’t shut the back pack. May your dust be forgotten, the end.”

Amry slapped Yo in the forehead and whispered, “Oh good great dragon poo. That was the worst spell I have ever heard in my life. May your forgetfulness be dust upon the heads of all frits present. Forget to shut your back pack. May your forgetfulness be dust upon the heads of all frits present.” Amry waved his spell feather around just in time to feel his hair growing and to see Junior finish shoving items into his back pack and not close it.

“It seems as though your home schooling didn’t stick. Who taught you spell speak? Onda’s mom?” said Amry as he smacked Yo on the head one more time.

Onda stood up, “Am, What did I tell you about talking about my mom?”

“You’re right bro, I was just kidding, but seriously, WHOA!” Amry was jostled back down into the bottom of the bag as Yo and Onda fell on top of him. Junior had picked up his backpack and slung it over his shoulder to carry onto the bus.

Amry tried to speak with Onda's foot in his face, "Now what do we do? I can't tell when we get on the bus or even when to get off. Yo, you better know how to get off this bus better than you know how to say the forgetting spell." Amry scooted Onda off of him and tried to stand up and hold to one of the loops inside the bag for holding pens and pencils.

"Don't worry Amry, I got it under controooooooh ouch. Junior must have sharpened this pencil before he put it in here." Yo pulled the sharpened tip of graphite out of the material of his shirt.

"Look Amry, I don't get off the bus until Junior gets off the bus. You'll see; this is easy." As they bounced around in the backpack, Yo began tossing out papers and writing utensils from the bag.

"What are you doing? Junior just put those in here."

"Well, it's crowded in here. I need room to move. I am a growing frit."

All of the sudden, they were thrown back against the bottom of the bag. Junior had picked up the backpack and was walking down the center aisle of the bus, towards the bus doors and then up the steps to the front of the school. However, he stopped for a moment to talk to a friend. He dropped his bag to the ground while he checked his pocket for a toy that he wanted to show.

"Get your socks on!" screamed Yo. All three frits scrambled to fit their socks over their bodies while trying to balance themselves inside Junior's backpack. Amry soon enough realized that they were no longer moving.

Jump!" whispered Amry, loudly. They all gathered at the opening that Junior had left in the side of his backpack and as soon as they jumped out, a loud ringing was heard through the air and many, many feet were stomping, stepping, hopping, and jumping over the steps.

A lady was heard saying, "Let's go children. The bell has already rung and it is time for class. Get a move on."

"Hold on a minute." The lady looked down on the top step to see three odd socks covering what looked like little clay figurines.

She scooped them up and carried them with her as she said, "These kids know better than to bring toys to school. If they don't want them lost or forgotten, they shouldn't bring them in the first place." She dropped them into a very large box right by the front door of the school. The box was labeled, "The Lost and Found".

Amry, Onda, and Yo stood up at the bottom of the box and checked their surroundings. Onda was the first to look over the edge of the box. "Amry, we're right by the front doors. All we have to do is wait for someone to come by and forget to close the doors; and we can get out."

Amry stood next to Onda and added his perception of their circumstances, "No, Onda, look."

Amry pointed to an adult who had just walked through the door and the door automatically shut behind him.

"Those doors have an automatic closer. If someone forgets to close the door, the door closes anyway. Look." Amry pushed Onda's head down a little bit and then pointed at someone coming into the school. There was a student running late and as he opened the front door to the school and walked in, the door slowly closed.

"Oh," said Onda, "I see. So we just need to move fast enough to get out of the door while someone holds it open for us."

"Right," said Amry, "Now let's go bring Yo up to speed. Both Amry and Onda turned to see Yo playing with a small stuffed animal puppy with a bright green ribbon around its neck.

Yo explained, "Aww, isn't this so soft and cute? I'll call him 'Goober' and take him with me everywhere I go."

"No you won't," said Amry. "We gotta go now and 'Goober' is not going with us."

Yo put the stuffed animal back down in the box and complained, "Well can we at least stay until the box on the ceiling says the Ledge of Grievance?"

"What? Yo sometimes I don't even understand what you're talking about," Onda said as he checked to make sure that his gear was still intact and in his satchel.

Yo tried to explain over a loud voice emanating through the hallway, "Well, every time I come to school with Junior, the kids all say this 'Ledge of Grievance' speech to the voice on the ceiling. I think it's about a landscape that is dangerous for the kids, and they have to say it every day to remind them to be careful. You can just hear it now."

Yo explained while pointing to the voice coming out of a small metal box in the corner of the hall ceiling. "It says something about knives and stakes that are under smog. That makes them invisible. I don't know. I've never understood it myself."

Amry grabbed Yo and Onda to tell them about an idea he had of getting out of the box. "Listen up, warriors. All we have to do is grab hold of the front of this box and rock it back and forth until it falls over. Then, we can hop out and head for the front door and get out of here."

Yo was obviously not paying attention to Amry's plan and was instead filtering through the contents of the box, shoving things in his pack. Onda conked him on the head to say *pay attention*. The plan was set and each frit had to make sure that their socks were on before grabbing the left and right corners of the front of the box. Amry grabbed the center, and as planned, all three frits pulled and pushed the box back and forth, back and forth, until the box fell over and all of its contents spilled out over the school floor.

A glass jar full of pennies and a bag full of marbles made a loud noise, as well as a mess, and the frits made a run for the front door. The administrator who had just picked them up and put them in the box stood up from her seat behind a large counter in the front office.

"What was that?" She moved around the edge of the big counter and saw that the Lost and Found box had turned over and spilled its contents. Her eyes followed the trail of pennies and marbles to the edge of the spill. Her eyes widened as she saw the three socked figures running for the door. "I guess whoever left those toys in their socks on the steps also left them turned on. Kids should know better than to bring their robotic toys to school." She ran to catch the three objects sprinting for the door.

Onda sneaked a look behind them to see if their plan was working. And indeed it was. The school administrator was headed right towards them.

"Amry," whispered Onda, "I know how to get her to hold the door open."

"Well then do it, now!" shouted Amry almost out of breath from running down the hallway.

Onda began to spell speak, "May your forgetfulness be dust upon the heads of all frits present. Forget that you checked to see that all the students were inside the building. May your forgetfulness be dust upon the heads of all frits present."

The Ledge of Grievance, as Yo called it, was just ending.

"...with liberty and justice for all."

The lady was walking towards what she thought were robotic toys heading down the hallway towards the front door. The frits, running out of battery power, if you will stood still in their socks, holding their breath.

Onda noticed his bangs growing, "Yes!" he exclaimed as the administrator ignored the "toys" on the floor and held open the front door of the school yelling, "Oh my word, is anyone still out here?"

Amry continued with spell speak as he and his friends headed out the door, and made the lady forget that she ever saw three odd-looking toys sprint down the hallway of the school and out the front door and onto the lawn.

The three friends stopped when they reached the teacher parking lot to the right of the school. "We need to get our bearings straight," said Amry breathing heavy as he took off his sock and surveyed the area around the school. "I remember Odge telling me that his father lived in a stone house with a three car garage that was three blocks away from Mr. Paul's automobile graveyard."

"We are definitely three blocks away. I remember Junior's mom asking him why he didn't just walk to his school that's only three blocks away." Yo replied.

Onda was looking around as well and pointed out that the parking lot was to the right and the school playground was on the left, and across the street were two large stone houses, both with three car garages.

"Great. Hmm. Let me review what Odge told me. Stone house. Check. Three-car garage. Check. Which house do we go to?" asked Amry.

Onda came up with another clue, "Well does Odge's name help out? I mean we are looking for a garage with a *Dodge* car in it, right?"

"Right!" yelled the other two. All three frits walked as swiftly as they could to the sidewalk in front of the school.

"Look both ways youfers," said Yo. "I don't want you two looking like the dead cat I saw on the road the other day when I found those keys and brought them to your interview.

"No," said Amry, "but if you ruin another interview of mine, *you'll* end up looking like that dead cat."

They looked both ways several times before darting across the street to the first stone house on the right. "Let's go to this one first," said Onda. The other two agreed, and as they walked down the side yard to the house on the right, they saw that it was definitely a stone house with a three-car garage.

Yo was the first one to point out that this wasn't going to be easy,

"The garage doors are shut. How are we supposed to get them back open? I could say the forgetting spell, but there doesn't seem to be anyone home."

"Does that remind you of anybody?" snickered Amry as he glanced at Yo licking on a marble that he had pulled out of his satchel. "Let's just go try the other house."

They walked carefully around the back yard of the first stone house to avoid having to put their socks back on. As they got to the intersection between the backyard of the first house and the backyard of the second house; Yo let out a squeal, much like a frightened rabbit.

"What?" asked Onda.

Yo announced, "A dog!" Amry grabbed Yo and Onda by the backs of their shirts and pulled them under a fishing boat that was parked in between the two houses. They stopped only for a moment to see if the dog was charging them.

Onda was the first to give his assessment. "Umm, Yo? The dog is tied up. Amry, we can leave; let's go check out the garage."

They walked around the back porch and peeked around the corner to check whether or not these garage doors were open.

"Hey look," pointed Yo, "two of the doors are closed, but one is open."

"Yeah," said Onda, "and that is a red Dodge sports car in the open garage door."

"Wow, how do you know that?" asked Yo.

"'Cause it's written on the back of the car," retorted Onda.

"Well that sounds like a car with Odge's name written all over it. Furthermore, there doesn't appear to be anyone inside. So let's go." They walked quickly through the open door of the garage and to the undercarriage of a Dodge sports car.

"Doesn't look like anyone is here," said Yo as he walked under the car and then in circles all the way around the car.

"Just because your child is born in the car, doesn't mean you have to live in it," said Amry as he began looking around the room. "Odge said that his dad lived in this garage and I just wanted to look in the easy places first.", retorted Yo.

"Well Amry, did Odge give us any more information as to where his father lived inside of this huge garage?" Onda asked while he started looking under drop cloths and bicycle helmets.

"Well, I remember him saying that he and his dad made their home in a box in the garage." Amry cocked his head to one side while looking around the garage. "And I'm guessing, by the looks of this place, that a box would be the only place for them to make their home."

Amry moved his hand over the room with a sweeping gesture to illustrate that the entire garage was filled with boxes: moving boxes, postal boxes, a tool box, gift wrapping boxes, Tupperware boxes, and even boxes used to hold catalogs and magazines.

"Was Odge trying to be funny? Amry, we can't stay here all day looking in each and every box for his dad. We have to be at the Great Oak by 10. Have we thought of how we're going to get back?" Onda seemed a little flustered and frustrated that Odge hadn't been more specific about where his father lived.

Yo decided to flex his opinion muscles as well, "Let's start looking then instead of standing around collecting dust."

Amry and Onda weren't pleased with Yo's play on words but decided to come up with a plan of attack to find Odge's father's box. "Okay, look youfers, we'll spread out. I'll take the back of the garage. Onda, you take the left side. Yo will take the right side, and we'll all start looking in each box." Each frit took his assigned position and meandered around their assigned area kicking, lifting, and punching boxes listening for sounds or looking for movement.

Amry searched his memory a little, "Oh yeah, now I remember. Odge said that his dad slept in the toolbox. I wish Tang were here; I can't remember what a toolbox looks like."

Onda overheard Amry talking to himself and came to his rescue, "Aren't they usually red or black with a buckle on the front?"

Amry decided that this was a good description for a toolbox and all three huddled -up to zero in on the new description of the box.

They all looked around for the box until they heard Yo say, "I found it! I got it!" Sure enough, there he was sitting on top of a red and gray toolbox with a big latch in the front.

Odge's father was an old frit, with a head of dust that led you to believe he wasn't in the presence of too many forgetting spells.

Amry approached him. "Sir, umm hi. My name is Amry."

Odge's father immediately recognized Amry. "Hey, Amry, from the news right? I saw your report about ElCa. That was something else."

Amry was only too quick to remember why the ElCa interview was so memorable and turned to Yo, curling up his lip in disgust, "You can say that again."

Yo responded, "What?"

Odge's father was definitely excited about meeting Amry who could be considered somewhat of a fritlebrity; and he couldn't help but ask a few questions'

"Hey, have you ever wanted to interview a garage frit, you know, a frit who knows a lot about cars?"

"Well, I'm not sure about that just yet, but I did do a report last night about a… hmm uhmmm." Amry cleared his throat, "A subject that might concern you, and I wanted to ask you a few questions to finish up the report before it airs tonight." Amry reminded himself that Odge was in the FPP, and not even his father should know his whereabouts.

"Sure, I've always wanted to help out with an investigative report or be interviewed on TV. What's it about?"

"Well, it is about the Key-pers." Amry watched the old frit's face as his eyes widened with the mention of that word.

Yo butted in, "We want to ask you about Odge's birth keys."

Onda knew what was going to come out of Yo's mouth, who was always inquisitive and impatient. He just didn't make it in time to clamp his hand over Yo's mouth. But he did have time to throw him to the ground and tell him to shut his dustpan and sit on one of the boxes so Amry could finish.

Amry tried to turn Odge's father's attention away from the commotion but to no avail.

"Does this have to do with Odge? What did he do? What happened? Is he dead? Have you seen him?'

Amry had to think fast. Odge was in the Fritness Protection Program and Amry was sworn not to divulge any information to anyone about him. Amry thought, and then decided to slow things down a bit, to buy him some time. “Well, sir…Wait, I hate to keep calling you sir. What should I be calling you?”

“The name is Benz.”

“Thank you, Benz. See the report involved an interview with some information that won’t be aired until tonight. So I am afraid that I cannot tell you anything about it. What I can tell you is that the investigation was indeed about the Key-pers, and we found out that your son was involved. So, I was just wondering if you could help us clear up a few things before the report is finalized.”

Benz’s earlier happiness at meeting Amry had faded into a scowl, but he let Amry know that he would be willing to help in any way.

“Benz, sir, I wanted to know…Well, I wanted to first *let you know* that the Key-pers apparently threaten frits who join their organization and subsequently, want to leave.

“Threaten them how?” Benz was appearing more and more distraught.

“You see…They ask, or rather, they demand to know the location of the frit’s birth-keys from the father; and then, they take them. If the frit doesn’t do the dirty deeds they tell him to, they place his birth-keys in the birth car’s ignition so the owners can find them.”

“It’s a death sentence,” added Yo.

“It’s sick,” said Onda.

“It’s probably going to kill my son,” said Benz. All three frits looked at each other and Onda clamped his hand over Yo’s mouth even harder.

"Well, that's my question sir. Were you ever approached or threatened by the Key-pers to find the whereabouts of your son's birth-keys?"

"Well no, I don't recall that. I mean, if I was threatened, don't you think I would have remembered that? Maybe they found them on their own. Half the time I am asleep in my toolbox. I may not have heard them come in." Amry was a little relieved but knew that he wasn't out of the woods yet.

"Okay second question," continued Amry. "If I might be so bold to ask, do you know if your son's birth-keys are still where you hid them?"

"I think so, I hid them really well," a smile returned to Benz's face as he ushered the friends over to the Dodge Viper.

"So can we see them, see if they're still there, for Odge's sake? I mean we don't even know if he's still alive." Amry looked over at Yo to make sure that he was keeping quiet about seeing Odge last night.

Benz seemed unaware at Yo's inability to keep a secret, and answered Amry's plea. "Well, you know, it's a funny story about how I hid Odge's birth-keys. I was looking for a great place for my wife to have our baby. I had two of my friends with me, Rang and Cadi, whose wives were also ready to have their babies. We were walking along this street, and we saw this three- car garage. It was open and had these three cars in it." Benz pointed to the Dodge sports car, a Ferrari, and a Corvette.

"It was perfect. The owners of the cars were cleaning out their garage. They had more boxes than this, if you could believe it." He pointed to all the boxes surrounding them, "And to our luck, they were cleaning out the cars as well and had left all three sets of keys on this bottom step." Benz pointed to a staircase, which led up to the inside of the house.

"Anyway, while our wives snuck into each of the three cars, I offered to take all three sets of keys and throw them into a box, filled with stuffed animals, which the owners were taking out to the curb. My friends agreed to be on the look out while I grabbed them, placed them in a box, and then checked on my wife. All of our babies were born fine, and in fine fashion, not too mention it only took a few minutes to find a great place to hide their birth keys."

"After we left the vehicles, we noticed that the owners were done cleaning the garage. The people soon noticed that their keys were missing. Oh they were frantic." Benz saw that Yo, Amry, and Onda were biting their nails. "Well, it does get crazier, I hope you have more nails to bite." The three friends nodded.

"The owners were smart. They started looking in every box, seeing if they accidentally tossed them into one of the boxes. I had made sure the box I threw them in was being carried out to the curb, and it was still out there on the curb. They hadn't looked in it yet. I kept my eyes on it the whole time in case I needed to retrieve the keys, but someone from across the street saw the box full of animals out by the garbage, picked it up and carried it with them."

Amry asked, "So, the keys are gone? You don't know where they are?"

Benz shrugged his shoulders and added, "Well I doubt that anyone has found Odge's birth keys unless they know where that box full of stuffed animals is."

Amry appeared frustrated for wasting time looking for keys that could not be found when he had other things to do that morning.

"Were there any unique markings on that box, or any other characteristics that might distinguish it from any other box?" asked Onda.

"Umm no," said Benz, "it just looked like an ordinary cardboard box. I am sorry that I can't be of more assistance. But if you do hear any thing more about the whereabouts or the health of my son, please inform me. I miss him. I really do."

"I am sorry that we got you worked up over, I guess, something that is out of your hands. Thanks for your help and make sure you watch the news tonight, you might hear something that could be of use to you." said Amry.

Benz wished them well, "Hey, youfers, you are welcome to come back any time. I enjoyed our visit."

Amry and his friends waved goodbye. They ran to the side of the house and sat down in the tall grass.

"Okay Amry, how much time do we have left?" asked Onda.

Amry looked in his satchel for the pocket watch and exclaimed, "Well, we're supposed to be at the Great Oak by 10 a.m. right?" Onda and Yo shook their heads in agreement. "Okay, well, we have an hour!"

"Yeah, well we would have had more time if you hadn't led us on some wild dust bunny chase." yelled Onda.

"I, for one, am glad we went on this little adventure because I found a new friend." said Yo who was playing with something inside his backpack.

"What did you take from the garage?" inquired Onda.

"I didn't take anything from the garage; I took this from the Lost and Found Box." He held up the stuffed puppy.

Onda continued, "You brought Goober?"

Yo started pulling things out of his bag, "Yes, among other things." he said as he pulled out a marble and a penny.

Amry pushed Yo's hands back into his bag. "Put that stuff away and let's focus on how to get back to the tree. We are running out of time." He pulled his pocket watch out of his satchel and hung his head repeating over and over again, "1 hour, 1 hour, 1hour."

Onda and Yo ignored him. Their friend had always been obsessed with time. They were used to his mumblings over his watch by now.

Amry raised his head and his voice at the same time, "How are we going to get to the playground in AN HOUR!!!!!" Amry fell backwards onto the ground and stared at the clouds going by. Yo pulled the stuffed animal puppy out of his bag and began pretending that it was barking and walking on the grass. However, Onda's attention was fixed on a white vehicle slowly moving and then stopping as it came up the street.

He got and idea and jostled his friends, "Amry, Yo, if we're going to get out of here, we better do it now. Come on youfers. GET UP! Yo, put Goober away, right now!" They all put their socks on and followed Onda who was escorting them to a large black pole at the edge of the front yard. The pole had a small white box attached to it with a pull down door.

Amry peeked out of his sock and began to stare up at the white box on the top of the pole, "What do we do now genius?"

"Just stay here, our ride will be here any second." said Onda as he pointed to the ground.

Amry and Yo lay still with anticipation as Onda peeked out from underneath his sock, anxiously awaiting the white car coming up the street. Soon enough, the automobile pulled up to the pole, and an arm reached out from the window and pulled out some rectangular shaped objects from the very box they were standing under.

"Get in." whispered Onda. This time, he pointed to the back bumper of the white car which led to a rolled down back window. After all three frits were in the back of the car which now began to move, Onda told his friends the plan to get them to their final destination.

"See, I watched this car for the last 15 minutes. It stopped at every house, opened the little box on the pole, took papers out, and put them back in. It seemed to be traveling in a straight path. So I figured if we found a way to get in the car, then it could take us three blocks down the road."

"Ingenious." mumbled Amry as he struggled to get his sock off. "Now, how are we going to get out?" Amry tiptoed up to the edge of the open window and saw that even though the car was moving slow, there was no way that they could jump out without being damaged. However, Onda had already thought this through.

"I guess we need to watch what this guy is doing to make him forget something long enough for us to sneak out undetected."

Yo peeked over the back seat to watch the driver who was flipping through stacks of papers and envelopes searching for the right addresses to deliver the mail to houses.

Amry moved away from the open window to see what Yo was so focused on and watched the mail man for a few minutes as well.

"I got it." said Amry, who had finally figured out what was the mailman's job.

"We make him forget to put the papers back in at the house which is closest to the playground. Then he'll have to turn around or back-up to take us there to do his job, and then we can hop out."

"Excellent," said Onda pulling out his spell feather, "Do you mind if I do it this time?"

Amry and Yo shook their heads, got back into their socks and awaited the time to escape.

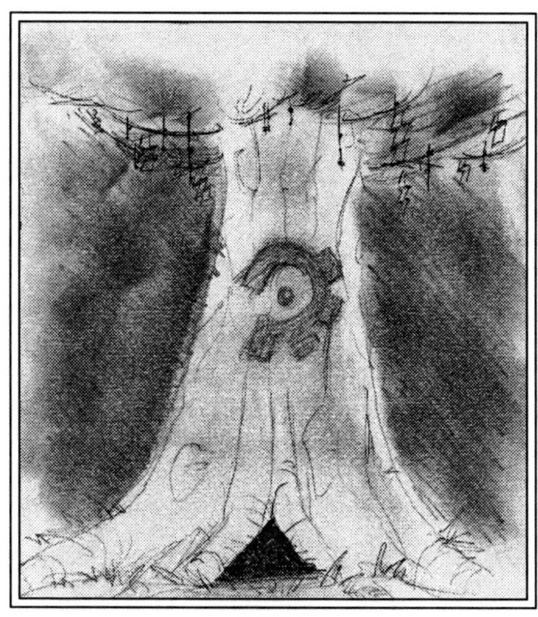

13

Fairies and Dwarves and Elves, oh my!

Their plan had worked. Onda made the mailman forget to place the mail in the box closest to the playground; but the spell didn't last long because the mailman looked down and saw that he still had the letters in his hand. No sooner had the mailman stopped back at the house closest to the playground then Amry, Onda, and Yo bounced out of the mailman's white Post Office car and headed on foot, in sock, to the Great Oak.

Onda was the first to notice that no child or parent was at the playground, seeing as the school day had just begun, so he told Amry and Yo that it was safe to continue on without the socks.

"I never thought we'd get out of these again today," Amry complained as he stretched out of his footwear, and then checked his pocket watch one more time. "Ten minutes youfers. Ten minutes. We are going to have to hoof it in order to get to the Great Oak in ten minutes."

He looked over and saw Yo playing with items instead of getting his sock folded up, "Yo what are you doing, put that stuff in your….. Hey?"

Amry took a closer look at what Yo had in his hand. "Hey, give me those. Where did you get these?" Amry snatched a set of keys from Yo's hands and looked them over carefully.

"Yo, you are a blubbering idiot; but sometimes, just sometimes, you are a blundering genius. These are Odge's keys. I'd bet all my seven years on that fact." Amry shoved the keys into Onda's hands to get his best friend to inspect them as well.

Onda turned the keys over and over and saw that Amry was right. There were two keys with the word "DODGE" printed right on them. Onda wasn't 100 percent convinced though. "These could be anybody's keys. There could be some frit out there named DODG who is missing these keys." Onda handed them back to Amry for further inspection.

"No, Onda. I know these are Odge's keys. Just think about it for a minute. Benz said that he hid them in a box with stuffed animals, and that someone from across the street came over to collect the box- i.e.: someone from the school. These have got to be his keys, and we're lucky Yo picked them up." Amry leaned over and rubbed the top of Yo's dusty hair which had grown long throughout the day's adventure and the spells spoken during that time.

Yo brightened up, "You mean I did something right this time?"

Onda patted his friend on the back as well, "It seems as though you just might have my little fritty friend."

All three friends moved as quickly as their legs could carry them to the large oak tree with a gaping hole in its trunk. They all sat down within the shade of the tree as the morning sun soon turned into near afternoon heat. Amry was an absolute wreck inside. He was so excited about finally seeing the Magic Forest for the very first time; but at the same time, he couldn't get his mind together to focus on the task at hand, whatever that was.

"Let's take a rest. I think we have about two or three minutes before ElCa shows up, and we don't want to appear ragged or dusted out when he gets here.", he said as he took off his satchel and helped Onda take off the sling filled with camera gear.

Yo cleaned off his vest and shorts and then sat against the wall of the trunk. Onda sat down too and made sure that all his gear wasn't broken from all the running and climbing they did that morning. Amry tucked into his satchel the keys that Yo found and as he did he felt that he still had another important set of keys with him. Amry silently reminded himself, *I still have to find a place to hide Icab's key from two days ago.. Hmm, I bet ElCa will know a place.*

Just then a cloud of dust billowed up from the trunk of the Great Oak. All three frits stood up from the ground and backed up to avoid getting a sandblast facial from all the blowing and grit. The cloud soon dissipated and the tribal leader of the frits stood before them. ElCa was wearing his usual tan linen robe with the leather rope around his waist, with his keys and spell feather securely tied to it. There was a scroll attached to his belt as well.

Amry noticed the scroll right away and wondered if it was a speech that he might give during the pre-voting vote meeting. He didn't have to wonder long. ElCa noticed that Amry was staring and confirmed his assumptions. He pointed to the scroll tied to his leather belt, “I am ready with my ammunition for the meeting today. Are you ready to do your first ever exit poll of the pre-voting vote meeting?”

Amry and Onda nodded in agreement, and Yo took Goober out of his back pack to show it to ElCa.

“Uh, that’s really nice Yo. Where did you get it?” asked ElCa as he took the stuffed puppy from Yo’s hands and proceeded to look it over.

“I rescued it from the Lost and Found box.” answered Yo.

“Curious,” said ElCa, “sometimes I feel like we all could use some rescuing from the Lost and Found.” ElCa dusted himself off and cleared his throat, “Before we head out into the Magic Forest, I need to set out some ground rules.” ElCa paused to make sure that they were *all* listening. “These rules must be strictly adhered to. We all know that magical creatures, including ourselves are very particular about rules, you know: spells, being seen, that sort of thing. In the Magic Forest, the rules are not as easily bent as they are in the human world. The gnomes are everywhere noting your every move and reporting it back to the queen, so you must do what I say.”

Onda nodded emphatically, “I heard about those gnomes. My ancestors wrote about the Magic Forest gnomes in their journals. They said the gnomes were serious, *dead serious* about their jobs.”

Amry jabbed Onda in the elbow. “Onda be quiet so we can hear what ElCa has to say. If we are serious about *our* job, we better get a move on. We only have…” Amry was looking at his watch again, when ElCa interrupted.

“Yes, we only have a little less than an hour to get over to Castle Court and educate youfers on how to behave in front of the other tribal elders.” All the frits simultaneously followed Amry’s lead in pantomiming an invisible zipper being zipped across their mouth.

"Okay," said ElCa, "you are in the Forest under my direction." He handed all three frits professional, crystal encrusted badges that said "Frit Tribe Representative". The badges also said "Leader: ElCa" underneath the previous title. Amry and his friends all attached their badges to their personal bags and satchels.

"Furthermore, you will walk behind me single file along the forest trail," He emphasized the words "single file". "Do not look at the other creatures that you pass; it will only incite their rage against you. Just follow the feet of the person in front of you. When we reach the fairy queen's castle, we will stop at the court in front of it. You will be gathered there with representatives of other magical creature tribes. Don't talk to them. This is not the time for polite, or impolite, chit chat," said ElCa as he gave Amry a stern facial warning with his eyebrows.

"What?" said Amry, trying to appear innocent.

"You know what, Amry. Sometimes you lose control of your mouth at a time when you should insert your boot into it. Just prepare for the questions you want to ask the leaders of the magical creatures' tribes as they exit the castle. Are there any questions?"

Yo raised his hand, which made both Onda and Amry roll their eyes. "Can I bring Goober?" asked Yo as he took the stuffed animal out of ElCa's hands and put it back into his backpack.

"Yes, Yo, if it makes you feel comfortable and keeps you from getting into trouble." ElCa took Yo's face in his hands and asked, "Do you think you can handle coming along and following my rules?" Yo nodded his head emphatically and closed the buckle on his backpack.

All three frits checked their belongings and told ElCa that they each were prepared to follow the rules and to represent the fritmunity well.

ElCa rubbed the key on his belt and brought it close to his mouth. The other frits did not hear what he said except, "Stand close my little dust bunnies and hold tight." Dust and dirt swirled about them and they were magically carried through the Great Oak and dropped on the floor of an emerald green forest.

Amry immediately scrambled through the contents of his satchel to pull out a little pencil nub and sticky pad to write down everything that he was seeing. He made sure to keep one eye on the new world around him and the other eye on ElCa's feet as he followed them and wrote at the same time:

The trees are terribly green, like fresh steamed broccoli

There are no leaves on the forest floor.

Who are the rakers?

Amry, again, looked up from his notepad just to make sure that he was following ElCa's footsteps. He did not even look to his left or right. He knew that ElCa gave the rules for a reason. But Amry decided that there could be no harm in looking straight up above him in the air. *Surely no magical creatures would be floating above him in the sky.* He wrote some more on his notepad:

Wow. The clouds don't just resemble animals they are the specific likeness of very specific animals.

Amry thought he was looking at a white dragon shaped cloud when SPLAT! A great drop of what looked like bird poop landed on Amry, Onda, and Yo, somehow bypassing ElCa. Amry grabbed the back of ElCa's robe to get him to stop walking and whispered, "What the dustpan was that, what is this?" Amry pulled out a handkerchief from his satchel and began wiping half gel and half solid white goo out of his dusty hair. He passed the cloth to Yo and Onda who seemed to be flailing just to get Amry and ElCa's attentions without making a sound.

ElCa started laughing. "I told you to keep your eyes on the ground." ElCa withdrew a napkin from his robe pocket, and wiped Amry's face. "Dragons slime creatures who try to sneak a look at them."

Onda exclaimed, "I thought dragons were toilet trained!"

Yo chimed in, "Obviously not!"

ElCa had to calm his troupe down before heading into the clearing at the edge of the woods. "Just clean yourself up, whilst I give a word to the wise. Dragons are very similar to birds. They occasionally squawk like birds. They fly like birds. They have modified scales which look like feathers, like birds."

Onda interrupted, "And they poop like birds."

Yo interrupted as well, "Do they have phones made after them like birds? 'Cause if they did, the dragon phone would burn a hole in everyone's pocket or jacket and that would just be dangerous."

"Yes Yo. The complexities of being a dragon would make it difficult to style them into a phone. Quite right. Now are we all cleaned off and ready to go?"

They all nodded "yes" and ElCa had to ask one more question, "You know Amry, I told you to keep your eyes on the path and now you have an eye full of poo. Do you think that you could be a better follower of the rules?"

Amry was quite embarrassed and realized his error. ElCa meant business; there were real reasons behind every rule. He finished wiping off his hair and brow and stuffed the dirty handkerchief into his satchel. He could hear tiny chirping laughter from behind him and could only assume it was either leprechaun or gnome. *Either way, I've been dusted,* he thought.

ElCa signaled for them to get moving; and this time. Amry made a conscious effort to keep both eyes on ElCa's shoes in front of him; which was hard to do seeing as he had never been in the Magic Forest and was longing to look around. He wanted to see where the elves and fairies lived, to look in caves for dragons and dwarves, but not this time. The walk wasn't very arduous or time consuming. *This is just one big let down,* thought Amry. *How am I supposed to be an investigative reporter if I can't investigate?*

It wasn't long before Amry felt the enclosure of the forest dissolving around him. They were indeed in a clearing. ElCa told the frits that they could lift their heads up now because there weren't any creatures around. The young frits looked around to find that they were standing on the top of a hill just outside the Forest, and could see three large hills in the short distance before them. ElCa drew their attention to the fairy queen's pink and sea foam glitter castle sitting atop of the middle of the three hills. ElCa noted that no magical creatures were larking about because they were at Castle Court waiting to plea their case or to hear other cases about statuses being renewed or denied.

"You know we are not the only magical creature that Queen Oletta banished oh so many years ago."

"How many years ago was it?" asked Onda.

"Well let's see. I think it was about 200 years ago when the Brothers Grimm assembled their Fairy Tales to be put into the world. You know this story right?" asked ElCa as they walked down Forest Hill into the valley of the elves just below the castle.

"Umm well, I guess, I, umm, we could all get a refresher course in frit history," stammered Amry.

"I only ask, because it's quite a walk from here to Barbahee Castle and you might not know all the facts."

"Barbahee, what?" asked Yo.

"It's the name of the queen's castle. She is big about formality and hoity toity high-to-do stuff, so she named it. Most important people name their castles," explained ElCa.

"Are you really sure you want to hear the story about our exile? I'm sure you've heard it a thousand times, or at least one or two times when I told it to you a while back." ElCa even sounded a bit excited to retell a story he had heard himself a thousand times. The young frits nodded emphatically.

"Around 200 some odd years ago, we (the frits) had what the magic world calls AMCS or Ancient Magical Creature Status." All three young frits rolled their eyes.

Onda exclaimed, "ElCa we know this already, get to the good part."

ElCa frowned at being interrupted and then gave a wink as if to say he knew they knew, but he was going to tell it the way he wanted to anyway.

"*Anyway*, as I was saying, we had AMCS which meant we had the privilege of living in the Magic Forest. We held many more keys to the magic within this kingdom."

Onda interrupted, again, "Like what? You mean we had more magic spells than the stupid *one* we have right now?"

"Yes, Onda. We held the key to the remembrance magic as well as the forgetting magic. We held the key to dreams as well. But all of this was taken from us just 200 some odd years ago."

"Where did we live in the Forest?" Amry looked back at the path they just walked through wondering if he would ever get the chance to explore it.

"We lived by the many streams and rivers that run through and by the forest. All magical creatures live in natural places that hold their specific magic. Did you know that all streams and rivers have memory? Even if their flow is disrupted by a dam or a bout of spring flooding, they always remember and return to their original path."

"Since rivers and streams are the places of natural memory, this is from whence we sprang and lived. Which reminds me, we also lived near natural springs and we were quite fond of making homes in wishing wells, which leads me to the next part of this saga." ElCa realized that he was skipping around a lot but he felt so giddy every time he returned to the Magic Forest and couldn't help it.

And Onda couldn't help interrupting a third time, "Hey ElCa, do we have to keep walking while we listen to the story, or can we sit down and take a break?" and before Amry pulled out his watch again, Onda cleared his throat and said, "And if you pull out that watch one more time and say we have less than whatever minutes, I'm going to make you forget you ever owned a watch!"

Amry replied, "I wasn't even gonna look at it, and besides frit magic only works on humans or other magical creatures in the human world, it doesn't work in here anymore. Sheez, Onda, don't get your dust in a ball."

The old leader cleared his throat, "As I was saying, well, first off, let's sit down, the meeting doesn't start for another forty-five minutes, and it only takes fifteen to get down this hill and into the castle courtyard."

Amry, Onda, and Yo, took of their assorted bags and plopped down into the soft grass of the hill and stared at the castle while listening to their tribal leader explain the rest of the story.

"Okay, I was saying that we were quite fond of wishing wells. Mainly because most wells are from underground rivers that have stopped flowing or have been trapped and it's just part of the magic that feeds us. Anyway, we used to grant wishes from the wells that humans would throw their money and trinkets into. Sometimes I think that is more fun than making people forget, but I digress."

Yo laughed, "Yes, I always wondered why you wore a dress."

"No Yo, I said I di....or never mind. Anyway Yo it's a *robe*. Most tribal elders wear robes as a symbol of wisdom and the lack of the need for more sophisticated attire." ElCa stood up, smoothed out his robe and sat back down. "Well, at the rate I am telling this story, we might need to walk and talk at the same time."

Amry told the other frits to shut their dust pans so ElCa could talk.

"Okay, anyway, there were loads and loads of children's stories written about us, and our wishing-well wish granting, our memory and forgetting charms, and all the funny circumstances and good that can come from the use of such magic on the human population. These stories were well loved and generally told over and over again at bedtimes and circle times, until the fairies came."

Yo added, "DUN, DUN, DUN!" as if to add evil villain special effects to the word "fairy".

"Yo, I said, *fairies*, not *Dracula*. Continuing, the fairies originally did not reside in the Magic Forest. They weren't exactly ancient either. Fairies came into being around 4000 years after we existed. No one is quite sure where they originated from, but some say Celtland, some say Wales, some say England. None the less, they came in droves. I guess they decided they needed the protection of the Forest. Apparently, the humans kept putting them in glass jars and mistaking them for large bugs. But, we welcomed them just the same, and we offered them MCS or simply magical creature status, much like the gnomes who didn't show up in the forest until after the fairies did."

Amry wondered, "Did the fairies bring the gnomes with them? They seem so connected, you know, the fairies being the rulers and the gnomes being the enforcers?"

"I guess I could assume that, but no one knows for sure. Moving on. The fairies showed up in the Magic Forest and not much was known about them. We offered them the protection of the magic realm and the status all the same. Around 200 years ago, there were some brothers in Old Germany, I think it's called, who were gathering up all the stories of magical creatures from as many humans as could remember what magic had been exacted upon them. These cases were rare and definitely merited writing down."

Yo asked, "Did they get stories about us?"

"Yes, Yo, all the wishing well and forgetting and remembering stories, they were all there. There were stories of the giants, dragons, and especially the elves. However, there weren't many stories about the fairies. It is said that the Fairy Godmother's daughter, who we all know as Oletta, was keeping a close eye on the news about the gathering of these stories. She was so full of pride about her looks, her magic, her meddling in human affairs that she wanted to make sure her stories were in the book. This is why she especially liked meddling in royal affairs if you know what I mean: very public and published."

Onda asked, "Oh, you mean the Once upon a time, there was a princess, or prince, or King or something like that?"

"Yes, Onda, something like that. Anyway, the Grimm Brothers, I believe it was, were about to publish a collection of stories called Children Stories or something plain like that; when they received a visitor that they did not expect.'

"Santa Clause?!" asked Yo as he jumped up with a smile on his face. Everyone laughed. Yo truly was crazy.

"Uhhhhh," paused ElCa, "No, the unexpected visitor was none other than Princess Oletta, daughter of the Fairy Queen, or Fairy Godmother. Anyway, the princess showed up to one of the Grimm brothers, Johann, I think. She asked him to see the book and noticed only one story in there, and it was about her mother. She was furious but still tried to get her way. She showed him marvelous tricks, or basically, she showed him herself, which we all know is soooooooooooooo against the rules of living in the Magic Forest."

It was Amry who butted in this time, "But what about all those stories where other magical creatures were seen. Weren't those cases against the rules?"

ElCa knew this would come up and had the answer, "No Amry, accidental sightings are perfectly legal or accidental. They don't count; but what Oletta was doing could hardly be considered accidental. She wanted to be seen, and she wanted to know why there weren't many stories of fairies. She wanted to know if Johann Grimm could re-work the boring title of his book 'Children Stories' to say, 'Fairy Tales' and include her story of her and her twin sister in a place called Foreverland. And if he was willing to include her story and change the title, she would offer him a one time safe passage through the Magic Forest and a collection of stories from the magic realm."

Johann loved this idea and was quite simply overtaken with joy at actually seeing a fairy. He agreed to the title, but not the story; it wasn't well grounded in tradition. Oletta then offered another condition. She wanted all stories that contained frits, eliminated from the final published work and Johann agreed."

"That overgrown mosquito!" shouted Amry.

ElCa placed his hand over Amry's mouth. "Umm, do you not know whose castle is straight in front of you? Don't comment, just listen."

"No one knows to this day why she chose the frit stories to be eliminated from Grimm's Fairy Tales, it remains a mystery; but nonetheless, it happened just the same."

Amry questioned his leader, "So, we were eliminated from a book, so what? How does that equate to being kicked out of our homeland? Why did we lose some of our magic, why did we have to leave the Magic Forest?"

"Well, the tribal leader of the frits at that time was Zebedee. I know it sounds like a strange name to you, but in the old days, frits were named with a name beginning with 'Z', you know the almost forgotten letter of the alphabet. They weren't named by 4 letter segments of car names like we are now."

"So, can I rename myself Zippo?" asked Yo.

"Yo!!!!" screamed Amry and Onda.

"Okay, Okay, I was just asking a question."

"Zebedee wrote in his journal that every magical creature, ancient and new, wanted a copy of Grimm's Fairy Tales. They wanted to see themselves in black in white, immortalized in the human world as well as the magic world. After reading the book, it was clear that every magical creature had a place in the heart of mankind, save one, the frit. And the title, 'Fairy Tale', well that must mean that the fairies are to be held above all, even though there was only one real story about a fairy in the whole book, and she was an old fairy to begin with."

"Zebedee was called to this meeting and his account is the only one we have of what happened next. This is when Princess Oletta became Queen Oletta. She told everyone she had a hand in offering up stories to Johann. She told everyone that it was she who checked the drawings to make sure that every creature's likeness was preserved. This is when the voting began. This is when Queen Oletta built the monstrous castle you see before you. This is when every ancient magical creature leader was invited once a week to discuss his or her importance in the kingdom and place in the heart of mankind. This is when AMC status was denied the frit for the very first time. The leaders of the elves, fairies, dragons, giants, dwarves, gnomes, all in the book, decided that since the frits were no longer in the stories; they would no longer be in the heart of man, and subsequently would no longer have a need to reside under the protection of the Magic Forest."

"They're all a bunch of toads." cried Onda.

"No, Onda, just the toads are toads. Did you know the toads are also seeking AMCS as well as us this year? Oh yes, AMCS is voted on only once a year. Of course there are the weekly meetings that I am allowed to attend, only as a respected elder, not as a frit. I even get to cast my vote once a year. Today however is the pre-voting vote. This is where all magical creatures seeking status come to plead their case for the final time and a pre-vote is held."

"So what are we waiting for? Let's kick some fairy tail," added Amry emphatically as he stood up and stomped his feet on the ground.

"No one will be kicking anything today. Let's go ahead and walk down through Elf Valley to the castle court yard. Oh, and you don't have to keep your head down and look at my feet anymore. All the creatures are at the castle, and we need to get there soon."

14

The Dust and the Pan

The sign said "Ellinvale" and as a precaution, this time Amry kept both of his eyes locked on the feet in front of him until they stopped and turned around and Elca said, "As I told you before, the elves have all gone to work. I think it's safe for you to look around."

Yo stopped and as usual was being curious, "Where do they work?"

"I believe they tend the gardens at Barbahee."

Upon hearing ElCa's words, Amry pulled out his pencil and again, began writing furiously:

The elves are gardeners?

The houses are all smooshed together

Everything smells like cookies

Amry's observations were interrupted by Onda whispering loudly into his ear, "Gnome! Look Amry, a gnome!" Amry looked up in time to see a figure dart behind a tree, a figure that he had earlier mistaken for a gnome.

"Ian," Amry whispered back to Onda.

"You mean the leprechaun that gave you bad luck, that's him?"

"Yeah," Amry replied, "remember I kept trying to tell you, but all the good luck and the bad luck kept getting in the way yesterday. Remember, he laughed at me when I fell trying to get my pass back?"

"Oh yeah, okay, now I see it." Onda stepped backwards to move further away from where Ian was hiding and tripped over a cobble stone sticking up from the pavement. "Oops, sorry." said Onda as Amry told him to be careful. He didn't want to give Ian a reason to start laughing at them.

Even after ElCa warned the frits not to lollygag, Amry couldn't help looking behind him. He saw that Ian was following them while ducking behind trees and elf homes along the way. Amry showed Onda and Yo where Ian was hiding.

"Cheese, he is sneaky. That really is a leprechaun?" asked Onda squinting hard to see a tiny green figure darting in between houses.

Yo pulled some small colorful bits out of his back pack and held them out with his hand. "Does he like marshmallow shapes, like they show on human TV?"

Amry was amazed to see Ian immediately come out from hiding and jump onto Yo's hand grabbing as many marshmallow shapes as he could.

"How ya doin' my fair sirs?" he turned around and bowed, while marshmallow bits fell out of his folded arms and landed on the ground.

Both Amry and Onda jumped back and held their bags in front of them to shield themselves from whatever magic this creature might possess. Yo, however, was a little less inhibited as he bent down while holding Ian in his hand and picked up the marshmallows that he dropped and gave them back to him.

"Hey there little fella. You dropped these. Do you want some more?" Yo opened his backpack to Ian who jumped right in looking around.

Amry tried to get Yo's attention by shaking his head, but Yo was very hospitable to Ian who seemed to be behaving himself.

"What else ya got in here laddie?" questioned Ian as he dug through Yo's backpack and began tossing out paper, pencil shavings, and a bottle cap. Ian's eyes instantly saw Yo's official press pass badge, given to him earlier by ElCa, on the outside of the pack.

"Ooh, this would get me into a fair few places, wouldn't it then?" said Ian as he unpinned the badge from Yo's pack. Yo was too busy being amazed to really care at this point and let Ian reach even further into the bottom of the backpack. Ian struggled a bit and finally pulled out Goober.

"Aww, what a beautiful fluffy pup. Its got a ribbon round its neck in me favorite color. I'll name it Shaunasee and take him everywhere I go with my brand new pass." Ian jumped out of the backpack, with surprising strength, dragging the press pass and the stuffed animal behind him until he vanished.

It had happened so fast that Yo had very little time to react to save his belongings from the leprechaun's clutches. Amry couldn't help because he was still in shock over the luck and misery that Ian had left him with the last time. He was afraid to do anything that might make Ian laugh. Onda and ElCa just took it all in; both knowing better than to mess with the locals.

Yo plopped down on the cobblestone street and let out a whimper.

Walking up to him and patting him on the head, ElCa tried to comfort him, "Yo these woods, hills, valleys, they're not like the human world. Everyone sees you; everyone has more power than you. It seems as if everyone wants something from you, but is unwilling to give to you in return."

"So are we here to get our feelings hurt and our stuff stolen?" said Yo as he fiddled with the closure on the backpack.

ElCa grabbed Yo's backpack, closed it and placed it on Yo, backwards, so that he was carrying it from the front. He tightened the latch on the front of the pack and whispered, "Carry your backpack this way, while you are here. In that way, you can keep an eye out for what's coming and going into and out of your bag."

The frit group prepared to walk up the hill to Barbahee castle, when they heard a French horn sound, "Duh-doo, duh-doo, duh-doo, duh-doo, duh-doo, duh-doo, duh-doo, duh-doo, duh-doo, duh-doo." ElCa was counting on his fingers the number of the horn blows. "Pick up the pace fritters, we've got ten minutes to get to Barbahee." He lifted his tan robe a little and began jogging and talking quite fast for an old leader.

"Here are the rules: Don't come in the castle. Stay in the courtyard. Try not to engage in conversation with the natives. Appearances aren't everything. Set up your gear and prepare for the questions you will ask the tribal leaders during the pre-voting vote exit poll. Ask only one question per leader. Understood?"

The young frits nodded their heads as they ran up the hill to get to the entrance of a beautiful pink marble hedge which fit together to make the shape of a hexagon. Right at the top edge of the hexagon was the front door to Barbahee Castle. At the bottom edge of the hexagon was where the troupe was headed: the gate to Barbahee Court Gardens, simply known as Castle Court. Within the hexagonal shaped garden were tall hybrid tea pink roses along the perimeter, which were colored blush pink and the stems were extremely thorny, to protect from stragglers who may want to clamber over the fence.

The frits headed around the right edge of the marble hexagon fence until they reached the front gate, which was just a patch of grass with a short and a long pink marble column on each side. Atop the two short marble columns were two perfectly matching gnomes dressed in glittering blush pink uniforms.

ElCa held up his hand to signal for Amry and his friends to wait while he approached the gnome guard on the right. "Captain Fendle, may we enter Barbahee Court Gardens?"

A tiny high pitched vibrating voice answered, "Pass please", at which point Elca held the Master key up from his belt to a box that the captain was holding out. ElCa proved that his key unlocked the box.

The tiny voice said, "You may enter."

ElCa turned back to Amry, Yo, and Onda and whispered that they only needed to show their badges with respect and then they would get in as well.

Yo whispered, "The leprechaun took mine. What do I do?"

ElCa whispered back, "Just stay here by the gate, I will see what I can do. Don't go anywhere, I'll be right back." Amry and Onda checked their badges with Captain Fendle who seemed to take an inordinate amount of time inspecting their passes over and over. He even bit Amry's pass to check the thickness of the paper it was written on. However, they were both let in, but before they entered the gate, Onda counseled Yo.

"Look, Yo, just stay here. ElCa said that he would see what he could do. Amry and I will be right over there." Onda pointed to the right top side of the hexagonal ledge, closest to the door of the castle. "If you really need me, just wave your hand and I'll come over." Onda patted Yo on the back and handed him a small box of raisins.

"Just eat these or count them, but don't move from this spot. You know that you get into trouble easily. Just keep yourself occupied." Amry and Onda walked through the marble column entrance and into Barbahee Court Gardens which anyone could sum up in two words: neat and pink.

Amry frantically looked around as if he might never get the opportunity to be here again. He quickly noticed where all the elves were and showed Onda what they looked like. They all had on bright pink uniforms consisting of short pants and a tunic that had a large "B" on the center. They were much taller than the gnomes, or the frits for that matter, and their large ears were very human-like except for a curving tip at the top edge of the ear. All the elves seemed to have very specific jobs. There were elves that only tended roses, ones that tended the fountains, ponds, mulch, and so on.

The frits were quite amused with the new sights and sounds as they walked carefully and quickly to set up a spot for the camera.

"Does this look like a good spot?" Onda pointed to a marble ledge which overlooked the set of stairs attached to the exit door of the castle.

"Yes, this looks great. Do you think that you can get all the gear set up? I know ElCa doesn't want me to make chit chat or anything, but I have to find out who is in the meeting so I can gauge with what degree of incredulity I can ask my questions." Amry grinned very wide and winked at Onda, who seemed unaffected while unloading the camera gear.

Amry walked over to the edge of a hexagonal shaped fountain and sat down on its ledge. Looking around the garden one more time he thought, *Hmm, okay, castle, behind me, fountain and garden entrance gate in front of me.*

"Hi Yo!" Amry saw Yo waving, and he yelled and waved back.

Okay, rose bushes to my left, rose bushes to my right. Hey, there's somebody. Amry saw someone talking to a gardener elf to his right. *Hmm, a member of the press maybe? A colleague perhaps? He may be able to give me the scoop.* Amry got up and began walking a little closer to the two who were talking to each other, almost whispering. Amry thought, *what kind of a creature is he? He's not an elf.*

Amry saw Yo waving again, and he yelled across the garden, "Yeah, Hi Yo. Didn't I already say 'hi' five minutes ago?"

Amry walked over to the elf and the other creature. He interrupted their intimate conversation, but not before he cleared his throat several times to draw their attention downward.

"Hi, I'm Amry from the Fristcovery channel newsroom, and you are?" He stuck out his hand expecting it to be shaken by someone, anyone. The elf ran off to the garden entrance, and the tall human-like creature stepped forward and looked down to observe what was surely beneath him.

"Did you say something?" he asked.

"Yes, I'm Amry from the Fristcovery News and I was wondering, you know, as a fellow journalist, if you could bring me up to speed on who is attending the pre-voting vote meeting and what they're like so I can get a feel for how to interview them as they exit."

"Why certainly. Amry, is it?" he said as he took the folded cape off of his forearm and flung it around his shoulders and back.

Amry could see now that the creature had two humps on its back underneath its cape. *Hmm, I guess hunchbacks are magical creatures seeking status as well.*

"What may I call you sir?" Amry asked the creature as it tied on its cape with a meticulous bow.

"Oh, um, Lancelot is what I'm known to be called on occasion, so that should suffice," he answered as he straightened his clothing and adjusted the humps on his back.

Amry seem quite pleased that Lancelot was being so cordial. "Lancelot, is it then? So tell me, do you know who is at this meeting? Do you know what they are like? How I should approach them, and all that?"

Lancelot stared at Amry for his lack of finesse in his speech, but then smiled almost instantly. "Oh, now I know who you are! You're that fritter, I mean frit, on the tele. You do the local interest stories right?"

"Right," said Amry, "and you watch that?"

"Well, most of us down trodden malcontent creatures do. You know the Magic Forest picks up just that channel. It's comforting to hear someone else blather on about the same woes we all share," said Lancelot almost forcing his smile back into a scowl.

"So will you fill me in on who's who?" asked Amry with his short pencil and sticky pad paper in hand.

Lancelot seemed very pleased at being able to help Amry with this information. "Yes, there is the divine Queen Oletta, I mean the divinely *evil* Queen Oletta. Then there is Master Dragon Ragule, who has the freshest breath of any dragon. It smells quite pleasant. There is King Gollywink who is extremely tall for a dwarf, and Elder

Snaps the gnome (who is hard of hearing, so you will have to ask his question, quite loudly, I'm afraid). Then there is the ever so royal Prince Ellinvaughn the II who is very short for an elf, with a large beard he keeps twirling. Of course you know ElCa, who is seemingly late to every meeting and talks too much. No offense, but I'm just being fair, right?"

Amry apparently didn't hear that last comment as he was still writing the name E-L-L-I-N-V-A-U-G-H-N.

Lancelot poked Amry to get his attention, "Should I go on or do your nubby fingers need more time to write?"

"No, I'm good, is there more?" Amry asked eagerly.

"Quite so," offered Lancelot, "There is the gargoyle captain, Grunt, who is one of the nicest guys you'd ever meet, and the pixie princess Buttertwerp who is supremely nasty and you should avoid talking to her altogether. It doesn't matter anyway; I'm not talking to any of them. They are all a bunch of royal pains in the knickers if you know what I mean?"

Amry and Lancelot continued to exchange notes on each other's opinions of the AMCS council and the possible outcome of the meeting until Onda came running over and grabbed Amry by the strap of the satchel around his chest and drug him behind a rose bush hedge.

"Have you seen Yo?" Onda asked frantically.

"Yeah, he's right over by the gate waving 'hi' to me every five seconds." Amry said.

"You idiot, I told him to wave if he had a problem." Onda was very frustrated.

"Well, how was I supposed to know that? I was getting information from this fellow reporter here to help me with my exit poll questioning. Now what's the problem with Yo again?"

Onda grabbed Amry and shook him. "Did that creature put a forgetting charm on you? Are you paying attention to what I am saying? Do you understand the gravity of this situation? YO IS MISSING!" Onda was bent out of shape and started searching around the garden.

Onda continued briefing Amry on what might be the cause of Yo's disappearance, "I think ElCa was late so he didn't come back to check on him. Yo must have gotten impatient and decided to hunt for Ian. We still have another twenty minutes before the meeting is over. Do you know what this spells?"

Amry grinned, he knew how to get Onda out of a twist "Does it spell T-H-I-S?"

Onda squealed in disgust and begged Amry to help him look for their missing friend. They first looked by the gate and there was no sign of Yo where they left him previously. They looked around the perimeter of the fountain and in the center of the garden and still no Yo.

They looked behind every rose bush, every ledge, until Amry looked up at the sky in disgust and said, "Well, he couldn't have vanished into thin air."

Onda looked up too and said, "IAN!!!"

Amry added, "Yes, Ian can vanish into thin air, but Yo can't."

"No, Amry, Ian!!" Onda grabbed Amry's face and directed his gaze towards the roof of the castle where Yo could be seen chasing a very tiny figure.

Amry screamed, "YO!'

Yo was chasing Ian the leprechaun. He ran across the roof of the castle, overlooking the garden, until he heard his name being called. He looked down and saw his two friends standing in the middle of the garden.

"Hey youfers. I'm getting my belongings back. I'm occupying myself."

Onda yelled back, "YO GET DOWN!!!" at which point Yo immediately started to dance some sort of Irish jig which transformed itself quickly into disco and then into head banging.

Onda moved in closer, shook his head 'no' and yelled again, "Yo, climb down from the roof. You could get us into serious trouble. Come down now!"

Yo bent down to pick up the backpack which he had laid on the roof when he started to dance and there just so happened to be a skylight at the very spot which showed a room full of magical creatures below it, in a heated discussion.

Yo spotted his beloved tribal leader ElCa sitting on the front row of a set of benches on the right hand side of the room, and waved to him. At which point, the proverbial dust, did hit the proverbial pan. Yo lost his balance and his flailing frame broke the skylight as he fell into the center of the pre-vote vote meeting room onto a large pink tuft in the center of the room. He had landed in the lap of the fairy queen herself, Queen Oletta, who was none too elated at having her outfit and furniture dusted on.

15

All in the Kool-Aid and don't know the flavor

Amry and Onda squealed with fear and rushed to position themselves at the exit door of the castle; which would certainly start overflowing with leaders, royals, and military figures at any moment.

"Okay, act cool, Onda. We'll do the exit poll quickly. Everyone who's in there will be coming out very soon. Don't worry about Yo either, ElCa is in there and will take care of him. Let's just do this." said Amry as he removed the microphone from his satchel and unwrapped the cord from around it. Onda plugged the microphone into his camera, and focused on the castle door.

The first person storming out of the door was Queen Oletta. As she walked out of the castle, she came up next to Amry, shuddered her wings to get the dust off, and in the process, smacked Amry in the face with them. Amry was knocked to the ground; but Onda quickly helped him up.

Amry straightened his vest to get ready for the next creature, as Onda walked back to focus the camera again. If Amry hadn't paid attention, he would have missed the tiny pixie, Princess Buttertwerp. She was about as small as Ian, and not too easily noticed with her natural toned clothing which seemed to blend in with the dirt and foliage of the gardens. Amry felt a tug on his satchel as Princess Buttertwerp was standing there pulling on it, trying to get his attention.

Amry recalled that Lancelot had told him that Buttertwerp was a nasty mean little pixie, and not to engage in conversation with her. So, Amry wiggled his satchel causing Princess Buttertwerp to teeter from the weight of the bag until she fell over. She pulled herself off of the ground and stomped away.

It was a good thing too because she barely missed being stepped on by the large stride of Master Dragon Ragule. As Ragule passed Amry, he bent down to say something into Amry's out-stretched microphone. He was greeted, instead, by Amry's nose trying to smell his breath that Lancelot had said was so refreshing. Master Dragon Ragule was none too amused because he thought it was being insinuated that his breath was not pleasing, and so he stormed away from the microphone without a word.

A very tall royal with a crown and pointy ears stepped out of the castle. Amry wondered if this was the unusually tall dwarf, King Gollywink. He held out his microphone and asked, "King Gollywink, as the king of the dwarf tribe, how will you vote on the

AMC status of the frit?" The tall creature snarled his lip, sucked his teeth, and answered, "How dare you," and then walked away.

Amry shrugged, *that could have gone better.* He prepared for the next creature that was approaching him.

He was short, with a beard, and also wearing a crown. Amry lifted his microphone to his own mouth and asked, "Sir, Prince Ellinvaughn, do you, as an elf, agree with the currently denied AMC status of the frit?" The short creature spat on the ground and twirled his beard as he walked away. Amry thought out loud, *"Lancelot was right. They are a bunch of royal pains in the knickers."*

Suddenly a growling voice came from behind him. "Who is a royal pain in the knickers?" Amry recognized the gruff voice to possibly be that of the gargoyle captain, Grunt. Lancelot had said that he was extremely nice and easy going.

"Hey Captain, could you be a sweetie, and answer a question for me?" Amry patted the large gargoyle's knee cap, and Captain Grunt flung Amry's arm off, which made him fall to the ground again. Then Grunt stepped on Amry's hair as he walked out of the gardens.

"Ouch, was it something I said?" wondered Amry as he tried to get up off the ground.

After leaning over to push himself up, he saw his very first certifiable gnome. *It must be a gnome. He's neither red-headed, nor wearing green, but he looks like Ian.* Amry remembered that Elder Snaps was supposed to be hard of hearing, according to Lancelot. So Amry began shouting to get Snap's attention, "Elder Snaps! CAN I ASK YOU A QUESTION?"

The gnome walked up to Amry, who was still on the ground, and shouted back, "I AM LITTLE, NOT DEAF, AND I AM NOT

ANSWERING ANY QUESTION FROM A FRIT!" And with that, he kicked dirt into Amry's face.

Amry spit dirt out from his mouth and mumbled, "That didn't go well at all."

"I'll say," Amry heard his tribal leader say from behind him. ElCa reached down, and offered his hand for Amry to grab to gain balance and pull himself up off the ground for the second time that day.

As Amry got up and cleaned his pants off, he saw Onda running towards them with all the gear half packed into his sling. "I can't get into the castle to check on Yo. ElCa , do you know what to do?"

"Yes, I do know what to do. However, what I am more concerned with at this moment is what *you* need to do. I need you and Amry to get this gear and yourselves off of the grounds of Barbahee, through Ellinvale, and back to the Great Oak at the edge of the Magic Forest, and I need you to have been there five minutes ago. Do you think you can get yourselves there quickly while I tend to Yo?"

Amry and Onda looked at each other puzzled. It was Amry who spoke first, "ElCa, there are a lot of trees in the Magic Forest. How do we know which one to go to?"

Then Onda asked his question, "And ElCa, do we run or walk? Do we keep our heads pointed at the ground, or does it matter at this point; because I am not trying to get a ticket from a gnome for doing something wrong."

ElCa drew both frits close to him, placed his arms around them, and spoke sweetly and softly, "Follow the cobble stone path through Ellinvale. Don't talk to any elves or leprechauns, or what-not. Stay on that path as it turns into a dirt trail straight through the Magic Forest. When the dirt trail ends, turn to your right. There should be a row of four or five trees. Inspect each one, for the Great Oak has two large branches emanating from the top of the trunk, and burnished on the underside bark of the right hand branch is the image of a key. Sit at the base of that tree. Do not move. I will be back as fast as I can. Look for my twister of dust."

With that, ElCa rubbed his key and whispered some words into it. A flutter of fallen rose petals surrounded ElCa, twisted about him, and carried him to the inside of the castle. This was Amry and Onda's signal to run.

They picked up each other's bags, and helped each other fasten them on tightly so they could run without tripping over their belongings and headed out of Barbahee Court Gardens, past the gnomes at the front gate, down the hill into Ellinvale, and back up the hill to the forest path. They neither looked up or to the left or right. They did not speak to any other magical creatures, let alone to themselves, until they reached the edge of the Magic Forest's dirt path.

Tired, worn, and a little scared in a dark unfamiliar forest, all could be heard was each others' labored breathing. After a few minutes of catching their breath, they stood up, and looked around.

"I wonder if ElCa has Yo in custody by now." Amry rested his hands on his knees still trying to catch his breath.

"Yeah, me too," said Onda, "I hope he didn't ruin our chances of getting our status renewed this year."

"You are hopeful, aren't you? Onda, the council has denied our status for the last 200 years. What makes you think they are going to change their minds now?" Amry plopped back down on the ground and began filtering through his satchel. He saw Icab's keys entangled with his microphone and pulled them out.

"You still have those?" Onda grabbed the keys from Amry and looked them over.

"Yeah, I need to find a good place to hide them, where they will never reach the ignition of her birth car ever again." Amry grabbed the keys back from Onda and put them back into his satchel.

Bored, Onda started looking for the Great Oak with the symbol of a key burned into the bark under the two forking branches. He saw four trees in a row to his right, and began inspecting the branches.

Amry sulked, "I'm never going to find a good hiding place."

"I know a great place to hide those," Onda held out his hand for Amry to give the keys back.

"Where?" Amry refused to give the keys back unless he agreed with Onda's idea for a hiding place.

"Right here," said Onda, as he pointed to the hole in the trunk of a tree with two conspicuous branches forking in the front with a key symbol on the bark.

"Good one," said Amry as he handed the keys to Onda, who then stepped under the right hand branch of the Great Oak to find a good twig to hang the keys on. He stood up on his tiptoes to reach a low hanging branch when he screamed with surprise. A figure had jumped out from behind the tree.

"Ooh! Ooh!" Onda screamed again as he ran backwards and shoved the keys back into Amry's lap.

"What?" yelled Amry as he fumbled with them, and tried to avoid being tripped over by his best friend. "You don't have to act like a monkey to climb a tree."

Then Amry realized just why Onda was screaming like a monkey. Standing before them, directly under the Great Oak, was none other than Odge, who didn't seem too surprised at finding them there.

"Hey youfers, are you doing the report on the pre-vote vote meeting?" Odge tried to start pleasant conversation to avoid being asked about what he was hiding under his tattered sweater.

"What are you doing here? How did you get in here?" Amry and Onda asked in unison, but not simultaneously. They inspected him for cuts and bruises and ultimately saw an odd shaped object stuck under the front of his sweater.

Odge's pleasant face turned into a frown. "Amry, can I speak to you in private?" Amry quickly saw that Odge was still twirling the bottom edge thread of his sweater, which he had been working on pulling out since yesterday's interview and also had a stick shaped object under his sweater which he was holding with his other hand.

Out of curiosity, Amry agreed and followed Odge behind the tree. "What do you need Odge? Are you okay? Have the Key-pers asked you to do something horrible again?" Odge began to pace and apparently did not hear Amry.

Amry tried to get his attention one more time, "Odge, look at me. What do you have under your sweater?"

Odge immediately turned around and pulled a large object out from under his torn sweater, which resembled a twirling baton with streamers, and two ends capped off with multifaceted quartz gemstones. He then immediately ran and hid behind another tree. Amry followed him and tried to get him to talk.

"Whoa, what is that?" Amry asked, hoping that Odge would be willing to come out of hiding and tell him. *Hmm, I bet I have just the thing to get him talking* thought Amry as he pulled something out of his satchel and dangled it in front of Odge, who still wasn't looking at him.

"Look Odge, I went to see your dad this morning. He misses you. I didn't tell him a thing about you being alive, even when we were looking for your keys. I thought you'd like to know," at which point, Amry jingled Odge's keys and placed them in Odge's hand.

"We found your keys; and we also found out that the Key-pers haven't threatened your dad yet."

Odge showed his gratefulness at Amry having his keys, by taking the keys and shoving the baton object into Amry's hands.

"How did you get these from my dad? Did he just hand them over? Does he think I'm dead?" Odge was full of questions, but Amry was too.

"What in the dust pan is this thing you just threw at me?" Amry held up the baton and twirled it through his fingers.

Odge took the baton back from Amry and explained, "Okay, I was forced here by Lord Vipe, you know, the Key-per leader."

Amry showed his disdain, but was willing to listen to Odge's plight. "Yeah, so. What is this thing?" Amry was losing patience with Odge. He didn't care if he was trying to leave the Key-pers, all he knew is that he got into the forest illegally, and Amry wasn't about to take the blame for it, especially since ElCa would be showing up any minute.

Odge looked over both his shoulders and leaned in closer to Amry's ear to whisper, "They want me to take it and hide it. I don't know what it is, but it can't be good. They let me in the Magic Forest with some special key, and they told me to find a place to hide it. I don't know where to put it. Will you help me? Just take it from me. They'll never expect that you have it." Odge shoved the baton back into Amry's folded arms.

"Listen, Odge, I got your birth-keys for you, but I think that's where I draw the line. I don't know what this thing is either, and I'm not trying to get into any more trouble than I already am."

Odge started to pull on the thread of his sweater so hard that the rows of knitting were vanishing quickly as the area of his exposed belly was slowly increasing.

Amry knew that Odge must be in terrible distress, and that the Key-pers could always find Odge and take the keys from him. Maybe he should help. "Okay, just, oh you owe me big Odge. Promise me you will find a place to hide and stay far away from here as possible?" Amry took the baton and fit it neatly into his satchel.

"Thanks for finding my keys, it means everything to me. And thanks for hiding this s..." Odge paused for a second and then continued, "this stupid baton. I'm not good at hiding anything, and they'll surely kill me if I come back through the Great Oak still holding it."

Amry was still unsure about the whole ordeal or what he was supposed to do, or how Odge was going to get back. "Hey, how are you going to get back?" And as soon as Amry had said those words, a flurry of oak leaves gathered and twisted around Odge which then carried him through the Great Oak.

This was good timing, because as Amry turned around to sit back down on the trail with Onda; two figures could be seen walking up the dirt trail.

"Uh-oh, here comes trouble. I can just tell." Onda leaned a little closer to Amry for support and protection, but in vain. Amry pushed Onda off of him when he could see clearly who was coming up the trail: ElCa and Yo.

The tribal leader was holding Yo by the waist to help him hobble up the hill through the forest. Amry rushed up to them to help Yo the rest of the way. "Is he going to be alright?" he asked ElCa who was lifting the key up from his waist belt.

"No time to talk now, we need to get out of here quickly. Everyone grab hands." And with that, ElCa held the key up to his lips, said something inaudible to Amry and the others, and a ribbon of oak leaves swirled up from the base of the forest, and wrapped around all four creatures passing them through the trunk of the Great Oak.

Amry let go of Yo and Onda's hands when they were grounded inside the trunk of the oak tree in the human world, right next to the playground. He stepped out of the trunk and into the sunlight shining on the meadow. He looked forward to see if any of the kids were on the playground yet. He looked at his watch, it was near 3 p.m.

"Hey, I don't want to be a kill joy, but it's near 3 p.m. and school kids will be swarming this area at any time. Shouldn't we be leaving or at least putting on our socks and saying the forgetting spell about now?" Amry walked back over to Onda who was attending to Yo.

Onda agreed that they should get back, "Look, Yo isn't looking that great right now, and I am no nurse. We need to get him back to Olet and the girls back at the salon; they'll know what to do with him."

ElCa agreed, "Amry, Yo was caught entering the castle illegally, albeit quite by accident, and that is a magical offense. The gnome guards were biting him on the ankles to keep him from moving. I had to literally pull them off of him. That is a crime as well. It might be well for all of us to lay low a while. I'll get you three back to Junior's house, and you can take care of each other there."

"Oh, and by the way, did you get any good footage to use for your pre-voting vote meeting exit poll report?"

Amry cocked his head to the side, and shrugged his shoulders. "There might be something that I could use, but right now, I think we had better tend to Yo."

They all grabbed their gear, and hands, one more time, as the dust lifted up from inside the trunk of the tree, wrapped around the frits, and carried them through the air until they landed right next to the back porch of Junior's house.

"I hate to leave youfers here, but I do have some important loose ends to tie up, if you know what I mean," said ElCa as he glanced at Yo. ElCa spoke into his key again, and was lifted up into the air, leaving the worry, hurt, and confusion on the ground.

16

If I knew then what I know now

"That was an utter waste of time." said Onda as he handed off his camera gear bag to Amry, put on his sock, and put Yo's sock over his head. He then lifted Yo over his shoulder, who was whimpering from his wounds. "Let's just get him back into the house and downstairs to his sister."

Amry lifted his eyes to the sky, and threw his hands up, "*You* can take him to Olet. I'm not going. She'll kill me for sure, or at the very least, find a way to give me a very bad make-up job or hair cut, while I'm sleeping."

Onda pulled Amry's shirt with his free hand, "You're coming and that's it! I'm not taking the fall for this one. Besides, I saw what Odge gave you, and you need to ask Wind or Star if they know what it is. They seem to know a lot about interesting magical items and lore. Maybe they could help."

Ford, the back door duty frit, had already made sure that the back door had been forgotten to be closed after he saw the swirl of dust come off the back porch. "Youfers come back from the Magic Forest? Everybody's talking about it. Something must have gone down, 'cause Ishi, down at the basement door, said that his friend had called him on his birdie phone to tell him that he saw a gnome, right here in the human world. They don't normally show themselves, unless somebody has done magic that they shouldn't have. Not only that, but this one is wearing *pink!*"

"Ford," said Amry, "mind your own business. Can't you see we've got an injury here? Call Ishi on his birdie phone and ask him if the coast is clear, so we can take off these socks."

Ford opened his black and yellow Oriole birdie phone, and dialed Ishi's number. "Hey, Ishi, yeah they're back. Do they have a clear shot from here to the washroom? Oh, I see. Okay, well they've got an injured one with them. Sure, yeah, we can set that up. Okay, see ya in a few." Ford closed the wings of his phone and helped the three friends take their socks off and put them away.

"Okay, Ishi told me that the family is downstairs flipping through channels. He is going to make Junior forget where he laid the remote. They'll be so busy searching for it, that they won't see you slip behind the couch, along the back wall, all the way to the game room, and into the washroom."

Onda hoisted Yo back up into a sturdier position up over his shoulders. Amry grabbed his satchel, Onda's sling, and Yo's backpack and hauled it through the back door, through the kitchen to the stairs which led to the downstairs family room.

Onda followed, but much slower due to carrying Yo. "Wait up, Amry. I can't go as fast as you."

Amry slowed down, waited at the top step of the stairs, and helped Onda balance Yo. "Fine, I'll walk in front of you, so in case you slip; I'll be able to push you back up. Just take it slowly."

They both saw Ishi waiting at the bottom of the stairs beckoning them on. They all heard Mrs. yelling, "Child, the remote is not a toy. It's not a block. It's not an airplane. It's not a slide. Where did you put it?"

Junior said, "I forgot. I just had it."

To which his mother replied, "Alright, well, let's take all the cushions off of the couch and start looking."

By that time, Amry, Onda, Yo, and Ishi were at the back of the living room sliding between the couch and the wall.

Ishi waved them on, "Hey, keep a look out for a gnome in a pink uniform. I heard one was lurking about."

Amry was too busy thinking about what lame excuse he was going to give Olet, to hear what Ishi had to say, as he walked along the back wall of the family room which eventually led to the washroom door.

Fortunately the washroom door was open. The family was so involved in searching for the remote, that they didn't notice three sock-wearing magical creatures skirt the back wall, and round the corner to the washroom door.

Onda gently eased Yo off of his shoulders. "You okay buddy? Do you think you can walk the rest of the way?

Yo nodded his head and limped ahead of Onda and Amry to the space between the washing machine and the dryer.

Onda and Amry lingered behind to formulate a plan of action. "Okay, look, let's go in there and act like it's no big deal. If we show fear and panic, then the girls are bound to follow. Let's just say that Yo got a little clumsy, and he needs some tending to. Deal?" Amry looked to Onda for agreement as they stood in front of the dryer sheet acting as a doorway to the style salon.

"Deal," said Onda as he lifted up the dryer sheet and walked through. "Oh, and don't forget to talk to Wind and Star about that thingy Odge gave you. *That* whole thing has me more worried than *this* whole thing with Yo. Deal?"

Amry answered back, "Deal! You follow Yo over to Olet, and I'll grab Wind and Star."

They walked through the dryer sheet, and were greeted immediately by Star. "I know you went to the Magic Forest. Do tell all," she said as she plopped all three friends into the overturned laundry detergent lid chairs.

As Amry landed on the lid, his satchel opened. The baton, given to him by Odge, popped out. It rolled on the concrete floor, and stopped at Star's feet, at which point in time; she fainted.

Onda got down off his detergent lid chair, and knelt down on the floor to revive her. "Now look what you have done, Amry. I didn't say to fling it at her feet. I told you to ask her about it. It obviously means something. She wouldn't have just fainted like that over an ordinary baton."

Amry also knelt down on the floor to pick up the baton, and Yo simply fell off of his chair for lack of energy to stay seated. Amry lifted him up, and propped him against the chair. He looked around the salon to make sure that no one else was watching the fiasco unfolding on the floor near the reception area.

Olet was busy with a customer, and Wind was organizing the wigs for sale on a counter in the back. Amry turned around to face Star, who was now revived, and who was glaring right at him.

"What?" Amry cried.

"You know what," whispered Star. "What are you doing with that? Is that why there are rumors of a gnome in a pink uniform looking for youfers?"

"What?" cried Onda this time.

"You know what too," said Star as she turned to face Amry, "Where did Amry get that?" Onda shrugged his shoulders and made a face at Amry to cue him that it was time to tell the story to Star.

"Star?" said Amry as he helped her and Yo back onto the laundry lids, "We were in the Magic Forest, and we were just about to leave when a Key-per in distress thrust this into my hands. He said if he didn't find a place to hide it before he was pulled out of the forest, that they would have his birth keys for sure. I told him that I would help."

Star stood up and began to yell loudly for the entire salon to hear, "No! No! No! No! Youfers need to get the cobwebs out of your fritty brains. You don't aid a Key-per, no matter how much distress they are in. Do you know what this is?" Star grabbed the baton from Amry and spun around to face Wind.

"Sister, they've taken Queen Oletta's scepter of power; that's why the gnome guard is here!" And with that announcement, a hush fell over the salon, which did not last for long when Olet noticed her brother falling to the ground for a second time.

She began to scream at Amry and Onda for their reckless watch over her brother. Her client began to scream because her needs weren't being attended to, and Wind and Star began to scream because their business was in jeopardy with such a powerful, and *stolen* item, in their midst.

The screaming ended with a bird chirping incessantly and loudly. "Will someone pick up their birdie phone for the Forest's sake?" screamed Wind, whose patience was virtually nonexistent.

Clients, employees, and visitors of the salon began checking their coat and pants pockets, until Amry yelled, "It's mine! I got it!" Amry walked out of the dryer sheet door of the salon to get some privacy.

"Yes?" he asked, wondering who could be calling his personal line, which only his two best friends and Odge knew.

A sinister, sticky sweet bass voice answered, "Amry, I presume?"

"Yes?" asked Amry again, wondering what stranger had his birdie number.

"I understand that you are interested in becoming a member of our organization?" said the voice. Amry walked back into the salon, just in case he needed back up.

"I am sure that I am not interested in joining any organization at this time. I am quite busy at the moment." Amry prepared to shut the wings of his phone, when the voice spoke again, louder, and less sweet.

"Well then, maybe I haven't made myself clear? It seems that you have taken on a Key-per job, and I understand that to mean you are looking to become a member of my gang."

"Who is this? Tang, are you playing a joke?" Amry retorted, hoping that it wasn't who he thought it was.

To which the voice replied, "Tang is indisposed at the moment; this isn't a prank. This is Lord Vipe speaking, and I would appreciate a little more respect from a frit who obviously wants me as his leader."

"Lord Vipe, is it? Well, I don't remember asking you to be my leader. I have a leader; we all do. ElCa, remember?" Amry knew this conversation was going nowhere, but he needed to hang on just a little longer to find out why he had Queen Oletta's scepter of power in his hand.

"Well, Amry, my dear, it seems as if you are unaware of how one becomes a Key-per, or becomes a mere speck of dust. Let me illuminate your way of thinking on this particular topic." And the birdie phone went dead. Amry looked around wondering what happened. He didn't have to wonder long.

A tall frit with broad shoulders, short dusty hair, and a striking face entered through the dryer sheet door of the salon. Onda grabbed Amry by his collar and whispered into his ear, "Uh, Am, I think your phone call has just entered the room." Onda pointed to the tall figure by the doorway who, as he closed the black crow birdie phone in his hand, introduced himself to Wind and Star as Lord Vipe of the Key-pers. He also introduced the two menacing figures standing guard over him as Ferr and Corv.

Amry closed his birdie phone, and sat for a moment watching from across the room, sizing up Lord Vipe. *He's got some size for a frit. Huh, look at that cape he wears. He's not a superhero. Are the tattoos on his face to make him look harder, because I am not impressed? He must not be too strong if he needs body guards.* Amry's thinking was disrupted by the quick swish of Lord Vipe's cape as he swung it over Amry's head to get his attention. Amry found himself staring straight into the faces of Lord Vipe, Ferr, and Corv: the three deadliest frits around.

"As I was saying, the way a frit implies that he is willing to help the cause of the Key-pers to dismantle the Magic Forest, and all of its inhabitants, is to offer their services to another Key-per. I am assuming you have met Odge. He told us, after we brought him back through the Great Oak, that you offered to take and hide Queen

Oletta's scepter, which he stole from her tuft during the commotion when Yo landed on her. How sweet of you to help."

Ferr and Corv bent over and grabbed Amry by the elbows and sat him down on the counter to make him pay attention to what their leader had to say. Lord Vipe dramatically swished the edge of his cape around as he strutted over to the counter and leaned in close to Amry's face.

"I have come to make sure you understand that this offer, that you have made, comes with strings. Should you complete the task you offered to help with; you will become an official member of the Key-pers, and obtain all the rights, privileges, and keys that come with said membership. Should you fail to complete your mission, you, in effect, are showing supreme disdain for the Key-pers, and you will heretofore become an enemy to the Key-per organization."

"No doubt Odge told you all about that." Lord Vipe removed his cape, vest, and belt. He wiggled his fingers through his dusty hair. He hunched his shoulders a little bit, and then began pulling a string from a dirty sweater that he was wearing.

Seeing this Onda pulled out a small packet of peanuts and sat down, "This is getting good."

"Oh no," said Amry. He tried to struggle away from Ferr and Corv, but to no avail. He immediately recognized Lord Vipe as none other than Odge.

"Oh yes," said Odge, who was undoubtedly Lord Vipe. "You didn't actually think that any Key-per would really get away from us, *and* be able to have a television interview, do you? Please. You fell right into my hands, and now, you will do what I say."

Lord Vipe pulled off a set of keys hanging from his belt. He took Amry off the counter. He dismissed Ferr and Corv, and proceeded to grab Amry by the vest and lead him to the other side of the salon.

"Dear, dear Amry. I would hate to see you turn to dust before your seven years were through. But I am afraid you have no choice in this matter." He waved the set of keys in front of Amry's face.

"What do those have to do with me?" asked Amry as he bobbed his head to avoid getting smacked in the face by the keys.

"Everything," answered Lord Vipe, "Do you see the writing on *this* key?" He separated one key from the rest on the keychain. Amry looked closer at the key and wondered how in the world Lord Vipe was able to obtain it.

"T-O-Y-O-T-A, C-A-M-R-Y," spelled Lord Vipe, out loud. "I especially like the A-M-R-Y part. These are your birth keys right? I will be placing them in your birth car's ignition. I don't know how long it will take before the owners of that car find their keys. So I would suggest that you find a very good place to hide that scepter, in the Magic Forest, before your keys are found." Amry tried to grab the keys from Lord Vipe but in vain. Vipe's grip was tight indeed.

"I'll give you a head start of about an hour. I hope you can find a way to get in." Lord Vipe attached the keys back to his belt, put his vest and cape back on, swished around his cape, and exited through the dryer sheet door; but not before he shouted one last detail, "Oh, and by the way, you should probably hide the scepter sooner than the time I gave you, because Captain Fendle, the pink gnome everyone's talking about, is looking for you. Just thought you ought to know." Ferr and Corv, his bodyguards, followed slowly behind him turning back to face the customers in the salon, checking to see if anyone was following, and no one was.

Amry sat there stunned at his own naivety. *How could I have been so foolish? I should have known. I wonder if I am still working off that stupid leprechaun luck and misery from earlier.* Amry walked back towards the crowd in the salon, all of them still staring at the place where Lord Vipe had exited.

"What's everybody looking at? He's gone, isn't he? Good riddance!" Amry walked over to Olet and said, "I am sorry that Yo got hurt today, truly. We were keeping an eye on him, things just got out of hand."

He walked over to Yo, lifted him up, and placed him in Olet's work chair. Olet, visibly upset, hugged her brother, and then said to Amry, "Do what you have to do, but come back safe. I don't need another frit that I adore hurt today." She kissed Amry on the cheek, and took her brother to the back of the salon to clean him up.

Amry opened his satchel to pull the scepter back out, when a hand reached for it. "Amry, I want to help you. I know a lot about this scepter, and I think I can get you out of this mess, but you have to promise to listen and consider doing exactly as I say," Wind held up the scepter and inspected it from end to end. Amry watched her intently, waiting for her to give any and all words of wisdom.

She let him squirm a little before letting it all be known. "My dear, as you know now, this is Queen Oletta's scepter. Its proper name is the Scepter of Power. Indeed, it is powerful. This is what she has used in the past to scoop up and remove power from creatures that she deems unworthy. She uses it to redecorate Barbahee every year and season. It's early Spring now, so I am assuming that when you went to Barbahee, it was all pink?" Amry and Onda both nodded as Wind twirled the baton between her fingers.

"You do not want to mess with the Scepter of Power. Its power can only be handled by its owner, which is probably why the queen has sent her gnome captain to search for it." She stopped twirling the baton, seeing that it was making Star, who had come over to join them, uneasy.

"Well, I am sure my sister has over glamorized this stick. Boiled down, this is merely a weapon. And even if I admire the queen for her style and taste; I do not admire her thirst for power over others. This is why Lord Vipe will never succeed. She will always find a way to have power over him. I bet he got hold of the scepter and burned off his hair, did you see that wig he was wearing? I bet it was more for protection from embarrassment than for a disguise. This is why he needs you to send it back into the forest. And you must; you don't have a choice." Star's speech became more rapid and frantic as she continued.

"And you must get your birth keys back. And you must avoid being seen by Captain Fendle, I heard he was an evil gnome. And you must...."

Star's mouth was muffled by her sister's hand over it. "And you must shut your lint trap sister. You are scaring the dust bunnies." Wind pointed to Onda and Amry who were shaking and cowering.

"There is only one course of action, and only one piece of advice." Wind made sure that Amry and Onda were paying close attention. She whispered into their direction, "You must get ElCa. He will know exactly what to do."

Her sister whispered too, after the hand was removed from over her mouth, "And you must go now. You only have an hour."

17

Scepter, Scepter, Who's got the Scepter?

Amry and Onda quickly snuck back to the Friscovery Channel Newsroom behind the entertainment center in the downstairs living room. They were immediately greeted by their boss. "Finally," he said with a tone of impatience. "I didn't think the exit poll was going to last all afternoon, let alone, all night. What were you doing? Were you asking all the council members their life stories?"

Amry sighed and responded, "I'd love to stay and chat some more, but we've got to get this report ready to go for the 7:59."

Ocus looked a little perplexed, "What do you mean? I thought we were running the perfectly good Odge interview that you gave me this morning?"

"Yeah, about that," added Onda, "That is rubbish compared to what we have here." Onda patted his camera gear in his satchel. "I'll run over to editing, get this one ready, and then I'll take it to Saab and get rid of the Odge interview." Amry pulled Onda back into the room.

"Are you sure we want to do that?" asked Amry. "Go ahead and file it away," he winked," 'cause I think we might be able to use it later."

They both waved goodbye to their boss and jumped up the input wire to the VCR shelf to the editing room. Ocus yelled something up to them; but they were too preoccupied to care.

"Okay, Am, I was thinking back there, this is what we're going to do…." Onda looked around to make sure that no one was around before he explained the plan to his best friend. "You are going to head out of here. Just make sure Ocus doesn't see you cutting out early. You are going to go straight to ElCa's to give him the scepter just like Wind suggested. I will meet you at your parent's house after the broadcast so we can ask you dad where your birth car is."

Amry and Onda hugged each other. "Aww Onda, I'll be okay; don't worry."

To which Onda replied, "I'm not worried about *your* hide. I'm worried mostly about *mine.* Vipe said that gnomes were after us for having the scepter, and I've read in my ancestor's journals that gnomes are creepy when they're angry. So let's just be careful, okay?"

Onda and Amry hugged one more time before Amry checked that the scepter and other belongings were tucked away neatly in his satchel. Onda waved goodbye to his friend and then proceeded to preview the exit poll interview.

Amry, devoid of much sleep as of late, left the living room, as he usually did, to go outside. For sometime he sat on the curb outside.

It was evening, so there was no need for a sock. What there was a need for, was a ride to the local library where ElCa lived. It was even further than the school and Benz's house.

Amry sat on the curb with his head in his hands. *How am I going to travel five blocks in the next twenty minutes? Dust it all! I need to be at ElCa's now.* Amry, afraid of being seen by the gnome everyone said was looking for him, put his sock on immediately. As soon as he had it on; he took it off. *Dust squared! I forgot. Gnomes are magical creatures too. You can't just hide from them within a sock. Think. Think. I need an idea.*

He could smell dinners being cooked and barbeques being held all around the neighborhood when the idea came. After jumping up from the curb, he headed to Ishi at the front door who was changing guard with Niss.

"Hey youfers," he yelled running up the driveway, and up to the cracked open basement door that the family used as a front door. "I need your help. Can one of you call Ford at the back door? I have an urgent request."

Niss and Ishi both took out their birdies, but Ishi made the call first, and handed the robin shaped phone over to Amry.

"Hey Ford, no, this is Amry. Yes, I need you to spell speak for me. I need you to make Mrs. forget to take the dinner out of the oven so it will burn. My thinking is that she will need to go out and pick up dinner. Yes. Well, I need a ride to the library and this is the only way I can think of. Sure. Do it now. You have your feather on you, right?"

Amry paused for a moment and apologized to Ishi for tiring out his birdie while waiting for Ford to make Mrs. ultimately burn dinner by forgetting it in the oven. Amry put the phone back up to his ear just in time.

"What? Already? Fritastic! Gotta go!" Amry handed the birdie phone back to Ishi, "You had better get out of the way. Mrs. is furious and is heading down the stairs right now. I gotta go. Thanks for your phone again."

Amry watched as Niss closed the door so he could make Mrs. forget to close it.

She did. She walked out of the door in a hurry, and without knowing the spell being feathered towards her; she forgot to shut the front door. She jumped into her car not even noticing the little creature that jumped in with her.

Amry leaned up out of the back seat window, and waved goodbye to Niss and Ishi as Mrs. started the car, and quickly reversed out of the driveway, en route to the grocery store. *Okay, now how do I get her to stop at the library? I can't make her forget to drop books off at the library, 'cause she wasn't going there in the first place. But….yes, this will work.*

Amry hid under an empty soda cup waiting until he felt like Mrs. was one block away from the library and two blocks away from the grocery store. He lifted up the cup and climbed up to the window to realize that the time had come to which he said, "May your forgetfulness be dust upon the heads of all frits present. Forget where you are going. May your forgetfulness be dust upon the heads of all frits present." Amry took out his word feather, and swept his spell towards Mrs. who was singing quite loudly to a commercial jingle on the radio.

Amry waited to see if his spell worked or not. *Was he too late?* He waited a few moments more as he looked out the window to make sure that they hadn't passed the library yet, which he could see was getting closer and closer. His bangs began to grow, and Amry knew it would soon be time for him to escape from the car.

Mrs. pulled straight into the parking lot of the library, opened the front door of the car, of which, Amry hopped out. She stood there in the parking lot asking herself out loud, "Where in the world was I going?" She looked in the trunk and the backseat of the car to see if she was taking anything to anywhere. Her stomach growled, and then she pointed her finger in the air and said, "AHA! I was getting dinner. Maybe I should get some herbs for memory while I am at the grocery store." She got back in the car and sped off.

Amry ran into the holly bushes which were on either side of the front door to the library which, by this time, was closed. He had been taught at a very young age where ElCa lived. All frits were taught how to contact their leader if they had ever been seen by a human, or what to do if they were in a jam. You were supposed to go to the library, and give the special flap opening to the DROP OFF BOOK slot. Amry proceeded as he had been taught.

He stood at the top of a holly bush to the left of the library door. He leaned over to the right as far as he could, and he pushed the DROP OFF BOOK door open one time really fast, then four times slowly, then three times. He waited for the elder to hold the flap open, and ask who was there.

"Yes?" ElCa's voice could be heard from just inside the flap of the book drop off.

"Um, sir? It's me, Amry. I need to speak with you quickly, most quickly." Amry looked behind and beside him to make sure that he hadn't been followed. He thought he could see a pink blur from behind a mailbox. ElCa unlocked the library front door, and beckoned Amry to climb down from the holly bush and enter.

"How can I help you, Amry? Has this anything to do with the Barbahee guard gnome that I hear is looking for you?" ElCa smiled knowing the answer already. He led Amry by the front desk of the library until they reached the card catalog: a large dusty dresser with tiny drawers housing many cards upon which the titles and authors of alphabetized books were written.

ElCa explained, "I basically live under here, sock-free. Since they put all the library book information on the computer, this large catalog is virtually useless. However, I always thought it romantic to be able to hold thousands of books' information in one place for you to thumb through. Anyway, I am going off on a tangent again, aren't I?"

Amry nodded, and then took a deep breath before he said, "Sir, I need you to take care of something for me. I was told that you would know better than anyone what to do with this." Amry slowly pulled out the scepter of power from his satchel, and sat it down on the floor in front of the book catalog.

"Ahh, yes. I was wondering if and when it would come to this." ElCa picked up the scepter, and attached it to his back with an extra piece of leather off of his belt.

"What do you mean ElCa?" Amry stood there with a puzzled look on his face.

"You are young and do not know; so I will tell you. The Key-pers have been around a long time. Their previous leader was Merc, but most frits never knew his identity. I did. I was like you, gullible and willing to help, until I found out the truth. The Key-pers don't do what they do for the good of the frit. They do what they do for power."

"Merc tried often to make contact with anyone that would help him with entering the Magic Forest to get a hold of the scepter of power. He made friends too, mostly fairies that liked ordering him to exact revenge for them on other creatures of the Forest. Merc never got the scepter, so when he retired; he passed his leadership to his son,: whom, I am sure you have now met."

Amry's eyes widened as he muttered to himself, *"Mercedes Benz, of course, Benz."*

"Oh no, ElCa. Benz told me where to find Odge…I mean Vipe's birth keys, and we found them quite by accident. I gave them to him before I knew his true identity. Does that mean that Vipe will live forever now? What have I done?" Amry sat down on the floor, and scratched his dusty hair.

"Dear little one, all will be righted one day. You shouldn't concern yourself with such things. Vipe is making you responsible for the stolen scepter which I am sure was given to him by someone in the castle when Yo fell. They probably knew Vipe didn't know how to use it, so no harm could come from it, except that the frits would be deeper into debt with the Fairy Queen than we are now. This would erase our chances of having our status renewed."

"However, I have a few tricks up my sleeve. You were right to come to me. I will take care of this for you. Now, I am to assume that your birth keys have been found by Lord Vipe. It is his modus operandi to dangle such a carrot before a horse such as yourself. You should go ask your father where your birth-car and keys are, find them, and remove them from your birth car's ignition. You can come back here for safety when you have them." Amry shook hands and hugged his tribal leader for his help. ElCa helped Amry out of the front door of the library. As he locked the door, he flipped open the book depository, and wished Amry good luck. Amry was just glad that his parents didn't live too far from the library so he wouldn't have to come up with another clever way to travel.

Back at the station, Onda reviewed the exit poll tape and saw the pixie princess come out first, and Amry blowing her off. He saw

Master Dragon Ragule breathing into the microphone, and Amry smelling it and making a face. *"Hmm,"* he thought, *"How 'bout I delete Amry all together in this interview, and just show the actions of the council? He'll look blameless, and they'll look like a bunch of stuck up, sniveling, hard-hearted creatures. It makes me feel better just thinking about it."*

Onda hooked up his gear to the DVD player, and edited the report until it resembled something worthy of being broadcast. "Right on time," he said as he carried the tape over to Saab in broadcasting.

"Slap it on, bro," he said. "It's almost 7:59, and this is a good one." Saab grabbed the tape from Onda and put it in to be played over the airways at.....

"7:59 Fritscovery News Channel brings you into the Magic Forest's AMCS council pre-voting vote meeting for the status of the frit. Amry had an opportunity to interview those who were in attendance."

The Fairy Queen sat in her throne room with a cigarette in her hand. Lance scowled at her and said, "Your Queenness, please put that out. It is ruining your fingertips from which all *important* magic flows." Lance tried to distract his queen from seeing news that would most certainly upset her, and it most certainly did.

She watched herself on TV shake her wings, and knock Amry to the ground. "Oh, fine, make me look like the evil one here. I was simply getting the fritty dust off of my wings. I was the one attacked. I was the one who had her scepter stolen. But do they put that in the report? NO!" Queen Oletta stood up from her throne and began pacing the room.

"Your majesty, do you really need to watch this? I beg of you, let's watch some of those decorating or gardening shows on cable. The Forest knows we need some new decorating ideas around here."

Lance pointed to the burned curtains and ripped up furniture from the effects of Oletta sparking everything in the room with her magic scepter when she got mad.

"Why is he interviewing that dumb ole' pixie first? Look at her, you can barely see her with her drabby clothes. Oh, and of course, Master Ragule has always got to push himself out in front." Oletta stopped pacing, and stood directly in front of the TV.

"Well, at least the elf, dwarf, and gnome got it right." She pointed to the TV when each creature spat or made a face of disgust at Amry.

The report was over, but the news anchor added, *"Apparently just as the meeting was let out, Queen Oletta's scepter of power was stolen. Be on the look out for..."* the newscaster changed his tone to one of disgust, *"Be on the look out for a gnome dressed in a pink Castle Barbahee uniform. He's searching for the scepter, and personally; I hope he never finds it."* Frit news never was that fair and balanced. Queen Oletta apparently wasn't attuned to this fact.

"Well, I've seen just about all I need to see. I guess you can keep a creature down for only so long before they start to revolt. Wait," the queen paused as a large smile crept across her fact, "Yes, wait, they were always *revolting*, that's why I got rid of them in the first place."

The joke made Lance burst into a little girl's giggle that made Queen Oletta conk him on the head with her crown.

"Sorry your highness, but that was a good one. What shall we do now? You can't just let comments like that go. Before you know it, the pixies, gargoyle, toads, and other ugly non-such will be questioning your power and start rebelling. Nip it in the bud I always say."

The queen retorted, "How about I kick you in the butt for daring to suggest how I should conduct my affairs at this point in time? You are a secretary, not an advisor." Queen Oletta fluttered her wings, flew to the opposite side of the throne room to the secretary desk, and removed the palace's birdie phone.

"Oh, and for your inside contact helping us earlier; he is a total idiot. Why you ever bothered calling Ian, the con, leprechaun is beside me. You give the guy a couple of marshmallows, and he turns into a one man Waterdance. If it wasn't for him, my left wing wouldn't be bent. All I wanted was for you to make Amry and ElCa look bad in front of the council, and leave me unharmed. Is that too much to ask for? Oh, but no, now I have to clean up your mess."

Lance bowed his head and muttered, "But, your royalness, I have a back-up plan in play."

The queen chuckled and said, "Yes, I know, you had better *back up* before I throw you out of Barbahee altogether."

Oletta picked up the birdie phone and dialed. She waited for a voice on the other end while tapping her unusually large, pointy foot. "Oh, there you are. New plan. Yes, gather a troop and chase him down until you retrieve the scepter. It's best if we use all the resources just getting my power back," she looked at Lance and returned to her conversation.

"Why do I need it back so soo… Don't question me! Yes there is some pressing matter that requires my most powerful magic" She glanced at Lance, and gave him the evil fairy eye, "I need to do some demoting, which requires the use of my scepter."

"Just come back, refuel, gain numbers, and then head back out. I want my scepter back as soon as gnomely possible." Queen Oletta slammed the wings of the birdie phone together, smacked Lance with her wings as she flew past him, and retreated to her bed chamber in the top of the castle.

18

Magical Creature Smack Down XXVII

Amry left the comfortable atmosphere of ElCa's library home to go to his own home. *Just wait til I see my dad. I'm gonna give him a what for. How could he? How could he give up my birth keys to the Key-pers?* Amry wondered and worried about his parents' safety as he walked up and down side yards, and through back yards, being grateful that most people in this neighborhood knew the leashing law for pets. His parents lived just between Benz's house and the library, so Amry only needed to travel about a block. It took him some time, but he got there safe and sound.

The house he grew up in belonged to a talk radio personality. Amry often spent hours just listening to the DJ practice his speeches, and yelling at the commentary on the news of the days events. Amry pretty much decided that his environment led him to a life in broadcasting, as well as a life of having to shove his foot in his mouth for his on-camera opinions.

He walked from the neighbor's side yard to the screened in back porch where his parents resided, along with a black tom cat named Slasher.

Amry climbed up the steps to the back porch, and then began to call for the big pet, "Ssssssssssssllllllasherrrrrrrrrr."

The sleek black tom cat purred at hearing his favorite play thing's voice. Amry reached in through a tiny hole in the screen door to scratch Slasher's ears and neck. He then whispered into the room, "Mom, Dad? Open the door. It's okay, it's me Amry." Amry waited for one or both of his parents to answer the door.

An older frit with stylish dusty hair, and a pretty apron print dress came to the door. "Dusty, dahling. How nice of you to visit." Amry's mom looked over to see Slasher purring from Amry's petting. "Well, someone else is also glad to see you. You know, you don't come around often enough."

His mom quietly and slowly opened the screen door to let Amry in, and to keep the cat from escaping as tom cats are prone to do.

"Aww, Mom, I'm sorry about that. You know I am getting real involved with my work, and you know you can always see me at 7:59."

His mom smiled as she hugged her son, and grabbed him by the hand to lead him inside an end table next to a patio furniture couch.

Amry opened the familiar door to his house and walked in, half expecting to see his father distraught and upset about being threatened by the Key-pers, but Amry's expectations fell way short to what he actually saw.

"Son, so good of you to drop by. Plop your dust on down, and talk with your father awhile." His father shook his hand and gestured for him to sit down at a checkerboard game acting as a table.

Amry pulled up two red checkers stacked together, and talked with his father. "Umm, Dad? I have a question to ask you."

"Did I see the exit poll interview? You bet your broom I did. That AMCS council is a bunch of outdoor broom hairs, if I ever saw one. How about that Queen Oletta, knocking you to the ground like that. If it were me, I would've given her a what for."

"I know you would, Dad. I know I wanted to, but that's not what I came here to ask you. I, well, I wanted to know if any Key-pers came to the house and made you tell them where my birth keys were?" Amry rushed through this line of questioning, hoping for his father not to be too angry about the situation.

"Son?" Amry's father looked quite perplexed. "Have you been hanging out at the salon too often getting a whiff of that strong detergent?"

"Uh, no," replied Amry who was now the one looking perplexed.

"Son, what have you gotten yourself into? You getting mixed up with the wrong crowd?"

"No Dad, look, here is the deal." Amry took a deep breath, and then proceeded to tell his father the entire ordeal. He told him of the ElCa interview, Ian the leprechaun, meeting Odge, the Odge interview, meeting Benz, going to the Magic Forest, having the scepter, meeting Lord Vipe, being threatened, and giving the scepter to ElCa.

"Wow son, that's quite an adventure for a young frit such as yourself, and I hate to disrupt this lovely, perilous, threatening adventure; but no one threatened me about your birth keys."

"What?" Amry leaned in closer as if he didn't quite understand what his father just said.

"Amry, no one came asking for your keys. However, I believe I know the riddle to your story. See, Benz used to be a friend of mine, 'til he turned to a life of dust and grime. A lot of us were very close back in the day. Unity is what we called it. We wanted back in the forest for our young families to be protected. So we all stuck together, had our families together, until some of our group chose to get back into the forest by means that I find frankly unfritly; so, we parted ways. Back in ought two, when your mom and I..."

Amry interrupted his father who was becoming long winded, "Dad, get to the point. Remember, I don't have a lot of time here."

"Oh, okay son. Don't get your dust in a knot. Here, let me call your mom in. She knows the story as well as I. LEXU!! Come in here." Amry's father cupped his hands and placed them around his mouth to project his voice out of the end table, and into the screened in porch where Amry's mom was enjoying some left over lemon-lime soda sitting on the table.

"Fini, why are you yelling at me? Just call me normal; you don't have to yell."

To which Amry's father laughed and said, "Okay 'Normal', get in here. Amry needs you to tell a story."

Lexu, Amry's mother, climbed up into the end table and pulled up two black checkers to the checkerboard and sat down.

Fini, Amry's father, told his wife all of their son's dilemma, and what information Amry might need.

She started off slowly so Amry could drink in the magnitude of the situation he was in. "Son, see our little family, and Benz's little family used to be very close. Well, until the falling out due to the Key-pers and all. Benz knew where we had you; it was next door to where he and his wife had Odge."

"Dad here says you went to Benz's house. Well, I'm sure he played it off like he knew nothing. He's a good liar, that's for sure. I bet he had your keys all this time. If you want to go and see if Odge, I mean Vipe, placed them in your birth car's ignition, go next door to Benz. It's a three car garage with a Toyota Camry, a Toyota truck, and a Honda Civic." His mother had barely finished a very poignant explanation of where Amry was born, when a scream came from the door.

"Sssssssssssllllllllasssssshhhhhherrrrrr! Get off of me!" Onda had his hand through the screen door. Slasher, like any good attack cat, was pawing and clawing at Onda to keep him from getting in.

"Come here Slasher. You don't remember Onda?" Amry grabbed Slasher around the neck, and led him away while Lexu let Onda through the screen door.

Amry came back over to the door, kissed his mom, and waved goodbye to his dad, "Gotta go folks, I've got some birth keys to retrieve and some Key-per dust to sweep into the garbage!" Amry grabbed Onda by the arm, and ran out of the screen door and down the steps of the porch.

"Let go of me, you big dust bunny!" Onda yelled, pulling Amry's hand off of him, seeing as he was still worn out from being attacked by Amry's cat.

"Touchy," Amry said. "Look Onda, we gotta get to that stone house across from the school. Remember there were two, side by side, that looked identical to each other, both with three car garages?"

Onda shook his head "yes".

"Well, that is not only where I was born, but it's where you and Yo were born as well. Isn't that neat? We and all the Key-pers used to live next door and play together."

Onda shook his head no. "No Amry, that's not neat. It would have been better if Vipe didn't know where we were born in the first place. What are we gonna do?"

Amry and Onda left the back porch, and began the one block journey to the house that Amry's birth car was in. Amry did all of the talking, as usual, "First of all, let's determine the parameters of our plan.

A.There is definitely a Barbahee gnome following me. You can't miss the bright pink "B" on its tunic, even when it's hiding.

B.We need to get to my birth car. It's in that three car garage next to where Benz is. Let me add, my parents told me that Benz used to be the leader of the Key-pers before Odge/Vipe, so who knows if he's on the look-out. Who knows if the garage will be open?"

"Let's stop for a minute.", said Onda. The two friends, who had been walking along side yards and through back yards had become quite tired. So they sat on the cool evening grass resting and thinking of their next move.

They heard a dog bark, and then an unhuman-like squeal. "Gnome," whispered Onda as loudly as he could while picking himself up off the grass.

"Yeah, I heard it too Onda. That's it! You're a genius!"

"What?" said Onda as he brushed grass and gravel off of his pants.

"Okay, tell me if I'm wrong here."

Onda, feeling a little more like his usual self after a short rest, said, "You're wrong here." Onda picked up his camera gear and chuckled.

"No, you big pile of dragon talon clippings. Listen, you said you knew a lot about gnomes from reading your ancestors' journals, right?"

"Yeah, what of it?" said Onda, picking his friend up off the grass, and walking towards the side of the house. Both Amry and Onda peered around the corner of the house to see if any bright pink was glowing nearby.

Amry turned to Onda and whispered, "Can frits make gnomes forget?"

Onda, who still looking for the gnome that must surely be lurking about, replied, "Not when we were in the Magic Forest; that's against the rules. You're not supposed to use your powers against other magical creatures." Amry tapped his nose and wondered out loud, "Hey, Onda, we're not in the Magic Forest, are we?"

"Nope," said Onda, who had just seen a pink glow from behind a street light across the street. "Hey, I know where we can get ourselves a gnome." Onda smiled and pointed across the street at the neon pink glow.

Amry devised a plan to get close to the gnome and make him forget. "If we get him on our side, Benz will leave us alone, and maybe the gnome's magic can get us into the garage." Amry was getting excited. He tugged on Onda to move across the street.

"Yes, but our magic only lasts for so long. Are we supposed to spell speak continually for the next hour?" Onda wasn't so sure the plan would work.

"If we don't do this now; we may never speak again," Amry pointed at his eyes, and then to the gnome who now knew he was being watched.

"Okay Onda, you go out and greet him. I'll spell speak behind this corner, and make him forget who he was looking for. Then we can *help* him remember."

Amry and Onda flipped their bangs to each other as a sign of luck. Onda walked proudly and boldly across the street to the gnome, who had just stepped out from behind the street light.

Amry quietly spoke the forgetting charm, as planned, while Onda greeted the castle guard in the middle of the street. "From Barbahee, eh? Nice duds ya got there. Pink's a good color for you."

Onda paused for a moment, hoping Amry had whisked the spell towards the gnome, before asking the important question. "So, what are you doing in the human world? Are you visiting a relative perhaps?"

Onda had never been more relieved to see the bangs growing over his eyes as the gnome replied, "Well, I....that is the silliest thing. I believe I have forgotten why I'm here. But, I have not forgotten why *you* are here. You're a frit and *not* to be allowed in the Magic Forest or Castle Court without proper identification."

Amry slowly walked from behind the house to stand behind Onda as he calmed the gnome.

"It's alright, my gnomic friend. I'm not trying to enter the castle. I was just trying to help you find Lord Vipe of the Key-pers. Remember, we were just talking about it?"

"Yes, well, lead me to him. I'll make sure to bring him to the castle. Wait, wasn't I looking for something else....the something of power?"

"Hurry Amry, say the spell again," whispered Onda as they walked back across the street, down the sidewalk, and towards the stone houses by the school.

Amry spoke the forgetting charm and twirled around whisking the spell words with his feather right in front of the gnome who asked, "What is your friend doing, a rain dance?"

Onda laughed, "Nope, just pest control. That's the way we frits ward off big smelly bugs."

Amry laughed as Onda continued, "You said you were looking for the *Deceptor of Power*, well that's Lord Vipe. We think he went this way; follow us." The gnome and the two frits hurried down the sidewalk to the two stone houses in front of the school.

Amry, Onda, and the gnome guard walked, talked, spoke the forgetting charm, forgot, remembered, and forgot again until they reached two stone houses with three car garages across from the school.

"So is this where the Deceptor of Power lives?" the gnome asked Onda.

"Oh, yes, I'll take you to him," Onda was grateful to see that Benz's garage was still open. He turned back, and whispered to Amry, "Find your keys, and then run like dust in the wind back to the library. Don't worry about me; I'll meet up with you later."

Amry walked up to the three car garages of the house next to Benz's. He approached the side entrance, hoping that it would be open because all three garage doors were closed.

"Aww man, could this get any worse?" And even though Amry knew better it still slipped out.

Accident gnomes were roaming around watching the high to-do castle gnomes chase after Amry until they heard the magic words.

He turned to his left to see an even smaller gnome than the castle ones – with an R on his sweater say, "Thunder and lightning, here they come. To say the magic words was pretty dumb. Rain and Sprinkle, wet you'll be, when you get caught by the guards of Barbahee, hee-hee-hee."

The gnome laughed and first pointed to a cloud over Amry then he pointed to six gnomes dressed in pink sneaking up the street. The cloud rumbled, and began pouring out rain.

Amry heard the bird chirping laughter of the gnome. "Just Fritastic," he yelled, "When will I ever learn to shut my big mouth."

Just then a small yellow truck was driving up the residential street, and started to slow down. Amry couldn't believe his luck.

Wait a minute. Was that an accident gnome or a leprechaun? Amry waited to see if his luck, whatever the source, would hold out. The truck pulled up in the driveway of the stone house with the *closed* three car garage.

"I knew it," Amry shouted as he ran to the back of the Toyota truck to see that all of the letters except for the "Y" and the "O" had been scratched off the tail gate.

Amry unrolled the wire from around his microphone, and lassoed it to the ball hitch on the back of the truck.

The driver had opened the garage door with a remote, and was starting to pull in. Amry scrambled up the rope to the liner of the truck bed. All the while, hearing shouts from the Accident gnome and the Barbahee guard gnomes, "He's getting away. There he goes."

Amry kept climbing, blind now from the pouring rain which had made his dusty hair droop into his face. KAH – BLAM! Amry felt the rain had stopped. The sun came out. *At night? No, wait. That's the garage light. I made it!!*

Amry almost jumped up, but realized he wasn't wearing his sock, so he laid down underneath a fast food restaurant bag in the bed of the truck. He waited until he heard the driver side door of the truck open and close. He hesitated a few seconds more, while the door to the house opened and closed, before repelling down his microphone wire to the concrete floor of the garage.

Okay, thought Amry, *Let's see.* He looked at the car to his right. It was a white midsize sedan with the word HONDA written on the license plate frame.

"Yep, my mother and father were right. So it stands to reason that…" Amry walked to the left, and saw a midnight blue, mid-sized sedan. Amry went to the back of the car to check his suspicions.

Alright, thought Amry as he saw the word CAMRY written in silver on the lower left side of the back of the car. "Yes," he said, as he walked over to the driver's side door of the car to see that it was slightly ajar.

Amry immediately became defensive and yelled out, "Who's in here?" and thought the only way that door could have been left open is if Lord Vipe had forgotten to shut it when he put Amry's keys in the ignition. *But who could make Vipe forget? Is someone on my side for once?*

Amry reluctantly climbed into the blue car, and pulled himself up to the seat. He stood on the leather driver's seat cushion, and leaned to the right to see if his birth key was in the ignition, and it was. He immediately struggled, turning the key to the right, and to the left, to remove it from its place, but it took him longer than he thought.

He could hear the shouts of the Barbahee gnomes getting closer and closer. He heard them say, "Well, he's in the garage."

"Can't you get that door open?"

"Not without the scepter. Captain Fendle was supposed to get it from him"

"Has anyone seen Fendle?"

Amry finally pulled his birth key out of the ignition, and jumped down from the driver's seat to the ledge of the car door. He climbed down from the ledge, and lost his balance just enough to land on all fours on the concrete floor of the garage.

Amry lifted his head up, ever so slightly, to see a surprise under his birth car. "GOOD SWEEPING! What is this doing here?" Amry recognized the object right away, and put it in his satchel for safe keeping. He didn't have time to examine it. The gnomes had stood on each other's shoulders, and were peeking in the door of the garage.

Amry had to move quickly under the car to avoid being seen. *How am I gonna get out of here?* Amry looked to his left, looked to his right, and saw his exit. There was a doggy door that led from the garage to the back yard.

"Bingo!" Amry shouted. He tightened his satchel latch, tightened the strap holding the satchel to his chest, and rolled all the way under all three cars until he reached the doggy door at the back of the garage.

Amry lifted the flap, and leaped out of the door. He walked around the back of the garage, until he reached the side yard between his birth car's house and Benz's house. He could see that the gnomes were still stacked feet to shoulder, looking in the door of the garage. Amry knew what he had to do.

He took out his word feather and began, "May your forgetfulness be dust upon the heads of all frits present. Forget what you're looking for. May your forgetfulness be dust upon the heads of all frits present."

Amry swirled his feather up and down so that his words would reach the stacked up gnomes.

He waited until his dusty bangs grew before he approached them, "Hey youfers, whatcha' doing?"

All the gnomes replied in unison, "You are not allowed in the castle without a pass!"

Amry smiled and said, "Oh, I don't want to go to the castle; believe me. So, again, why are youfers here?"

The gnomes jumped down, one by one, and faced Amry without responding.

"Oh yes," he said, "Youfers were looking for Fendle. I saw him. He went into the garden back here. I guess he got hungry. Do you want to come and see?"

The line of gnomes followed Amry to the backyard, where a small fenced in garden was in the center.

Amry walked up to the gate, and used his birth key from his satchel to pry open the latch on the gate. He beckoned the gnomes to enter through the gate. When the last one went through, Amry yelled, "I saw your captain in the back, picking tomatoes. Go and see."

The gnomes ran to the back of the garden. Amry quickly shut and latched the garden gate, and reminded himself that his spell would wear off soon; so he better get a move on.

He had barely passed the garage of the stone house when he heard the gnomes say, "He's getting away!! Let's get this gate unlatched NOW!!"

He ran as fast as his short little legs could take him *It's only two blocks from here to the library. I can make that...even if it takes me all night.* Amry ran across the street to go around the school. Around the school he went, past the front steps, around the side to the basketball court, and around the back to the kickball field where he stopped to rest.

This is going to take forever. The field was so still and quiet that Amry could hear his heavy breathing, until it was interrupted by someone shouting.

"RUN, AMRY, RUN!" Amry to his surprise, and relief, saw Onda running towards his yelling, "They're pink; they're mad, and there are definitely more of them now."

As Onda passed him, he grabbed his vest and pulled him to a jogging position. "Let's go – NOW – They're chasing us." Amry turned to see a pink streak of light headed right towards them.

They ran in circles around the school for what seemed like hours. The gnomes chased them around the house in front of the library for another several hours. The sun was starting to come up when Onda pulled out his word feather, and said the forgetting spell to get the gnomes to forget why they were running.

The gnomes stopped in their tracks for a few moments; forgetting and wondering just long enough for Onda and Amry to sprint across the street to the library.

Amry watched Onda flip the Book Drop door open, one, then four, then three times. Amry followed after, climbing up the holly bush, and leaning toward the Book Drop.

FLAP. Amry almost lost his footing. FLAP, FLAP, FLAP, FLAP. *Home free,* thought Amry. FLAP, FLAP, FL.... He tried to flap the last time, but something had grabbed his foot, and was pulling him back towards the bush.

Amry turned, expecting to see a Barbahee gnome, but was instead greeted by Ferr and Corv, Lord Vipe's henchmen. "Let go!" Amry screamed to no avail. Amry held tight to the lip of the book drop flap. "Help," he screamed as Ferr and Corv started to pull on him to make him let go.

Amry felt a hand touch his hand, as he turned back to watch Ferr and Corv pull even harder.

"I am helping," Amry heard someone say and he turned to see ElCa wave his word feather out the flap and towards Ferr and Corv, who soon let go of Amry.

They climbed down off of the holly bush, wondering why they were even there.

ElCa quickly pulled Amry through the book flap and onto the cold floor of the library foyer.

19

Finders Keepers Losers Weepers

"What a mess," said Amry as he tried to catch his breath, and looked around at the card catalog dresser where ElCa lived.

The cards were all flipped out and strewn all over the library. The drawers to the catalog were open, and ElCa's bed under the catalog was overturned.

"Gnomes?" yelled Onda with exasperation. He too was trying to catch his breath, and felt he knew who could've done this sort of thing. ElCa began picking up cards and hopping from drawer to drawer, replacing them in their proper place.

As he scooped up three cards he replied, "Nope, Vipe."

"What!?" said Amry as he began studying the room looking for clues that might have led ElCa to that conclusion.

"I'm pretty sure it was Vipe," said ElCa. "He took the scepter of power, and he took my birth key. Both of which are pretty good bargaining chips, but only a frit would have taken my birth key."

Amry and Onda agreed, and further agreed that an exchange was in order. They spent the rest of the early morning helping ElCa clean up before the library staff arrived and devising a plan to get the scepter and ElCa's birth key, back.

"Listen up you two, thanks for helping. Your kindness is appreciated. Secondly, don't worry about me." ElCa sat both of the frits down under the card catalog to give more counsel.

"What you need to understand is that my time has come. My seven years have come and gone. Vipe having my birth key isn't a big deal. If I go; it's my time. What's important is that the scepter gets back to the Queen before we lose all credibility and *hope* of regaining status."

On the other side of the neighborhood, the Fairy Queen's gnome army returned through the Great Oak, and marched down the hill through Ellinvale, and back up the hill to Barbahee. They were greeted by the queen herself at the center of Barbahee Court.

"Captain Fendle, Lieutenant Jones, am I to suspect by your weary faces and defeated appearances that you neither have a prisoner nor the scepter of power?"

Captain Fendle answered, "Your majesty, I take full responsibility. I did not realize that the frits could use their magic on us in the human world. My memory right now is a little fuzzy."

The queen placed her hand over Captain Fendle's mouth to get him to stop talking. "Yes, well, how about I make your body fuzzy to go with that memory of yours."

Blue sparks shot from the queen's fingertips, and Captain Fendle was magically transformed into a rabbit. The gnome army fell to the ground and worshipped their queen in hopes that this act might dispel any other inkling that the queen might have to turn the rest of them into tiny furry creatures.

She paced back and forth in front of the gnome army line, flitting her wings every three steps. She stopped in front of Lieutenant Jones. She lifted him up off the ground and spoke, "Lieutenant, you are hereby, and forthwith, Captain Jones of the gnome guard. I am assuming that, in the future, you will not forget the capabilities of the frit within, and without, the protection of the forest." He replied, "Yes, your majesty, your grace, your most fair, and thin, and beautiful."

The queen gave the word for all the gnomes to get up off the ground, "Yes, well, flattery gets you everywhere. Stop groveling, and get back to the castle. I need you to set up another battle plan should I desire to use your services in the human world again." She fluttered her wings, lifted off of the ground, and flew to a second story window of the castle. She met Lance in the throne room. He was preparing the queen's favorite lunch: a chilled, fat free, sugar free, taste free moss soup in the hopes that she would forgive him and allow him to put his back up plan into play.

"Your highness, you look so thin. I have made you a light lunch, your favorite. I have also prepared a little presentation for you."

The queen sat down at a long table and waited for Lance to bring her chilled soup. "What is this little 'presentation'?" the queen asked.

Lance replied, "Well, don't be alarmed; I just brought him in as a last resort. You can use him or not, it's up to you." Lance retreated to a curtain at the front of the room and beckoned a creature to step forward.

"Your majesty, I'd like to present to you Lord Vipe, head of the Key-pers."

"Oh yes," the queen put her soup spoon down, and focused her attention on the frit. "I saw a short report on your organization on the Fritscovery News Channel. What can your organization offer me?"

"Your queeness, I come with news. I have your scepter. I also have ElCa in a tight spot."

The queen responded, "Well, I am not fond about number one, but number two sounds promising. Did you bring my scepter with you?"

"Oh no, your majesty, it's waiting outside, should you agree to my request. I would expect that you would understand the beauty in that. You now need me as much as I need you."

Oletta laughed, "That might be but for a small moment in your little life, but let's continue."

"Your most high fairy," said Vipe as he sat down at the table, uninvited to do so. "I need your magical talents. ElCa, as you know, is the leader of the frits and has been a thorn in my side for quite some time. I would be running the tribe of frits by now, if it weren't for his rightful position as leader because he holds the master key. I need magic. I need a spell to get rid of him once and for all."

"I have his birth key, to place in his birth car. His father is long dead, and I can't find the car he was born in. I have no idea how to get him out of the picture, and get myself into it." The queen smiled an evil smile with an evil glint in her eyes. She stood up from the long table, walked over to Vipe, lifted him out of the chair by the elbow, and escorted him to a seat by her throne. "So that is how you frits have been skirting my curse, interesting, very interesting. I can see that I truly do need you. ElCa has been a thorn in my side as well. I would love to stop having these superfluous council meetings, and I would love to be able to have someone I can con.....converse with on a regular basis about the human world."

The queen stuttered on the word "converse" as she was going to say "control", but did not want to scare off the dirty creature. "Walk with me," she asked him as she led him to Barbahee Gardens.

As Lord Vipe walked with Queen Oletta, so did Amry walk with Onda, right to the editing room of the Fritscovery News offices.

"Okay, now what?" asked Onda who took the sling from off of his chest which was holding his camera gear. He had been running in circles around the neighborhood with it on all night. Amry took off his satchel, and emptied out its contents. "Dust it all," yelled Amry as he studied the contents of his bag.

"What?" asked Onda.

"I left my microphone in the back of Yo's birth truck. I think I am going to need to get a new one for what I have planned. Is there still battery life left in your camera, or do you need to charge it?"

"What for?" asked Onda, who watched nervously as Amry treaded a straight line into the VCR shelf, as he walked back and forth scratching his dust.

"Okay. Let's review. Vipe has the scepter. Vipe has ElCa's birth keys. I have my birth keys. I have Vipe's birth keys, I even still have Icab's birth keys. Hey?" Amry's eyes widened and a smile crept on his face.

"You have Vipe's keys?" Onda was puzzled.

"It's the strangest thing," said Amry. "I went looking for my keys, that Vipe had stolen, and I end up finding them *and* Vipe's keys as well. They were laying on the garage floor right under my birth car. If anyone is a Key-per, I am. Onda, I've got it." Amry tapped his friend on the shoulder to get his attention.

"Got what? A serious dust disorder? Yes, I am inclined to agree."

"No, Onda. I know what to do. Charge your camera, get it ready. Also, retrieve that old Odge interview. I want to run it tonight with some modification."

Onda and Amry spent the rest of the afternoon finding an extra microphone, and talking to Ocus for approval to run the Odge interview that night at 7:59.

Meanwhile, the Fairy Queen followed Lord Vipe to the edge of the Magic Forest at the Great Oak and asked, "So, are we clear on the plan?" She put her hands on her hips to prepare for disapproval if this frit turned out to be as forgetful as her gnomes.

"Yes your highness, should I recite?"

"Anytime," she added as she tapped her long, pointy fairy foot.

"Okay, I go and get your scepter. I bring it back. You take ElCa's key from me, and tap it with your scepter, which will make it reveal what it unlocks. Right?"

"For once," the queen responded, "Now go, and do!"

Lord Vipe turned his back to the queen as he prepared to be whisked back through the Great Oak. He pulled out a key from the back of his Key-per badge that he wore on the left shoulder of his cape. It was handed to him from his father, and to his father from his father and so on, and so on, back 200 years.

It fit perfectly into the burnished key shape in the bark of the Great Oak. Lord Vipe placed the key in the bark under the right branch of the tree, and waited for dust to engulf him, and carry him through. When he was finally through the Great Oak, he saw his two accomplices sitting on the floor of the tree, cleaning dirty pieces of what looked like gold.

"What is that you have there?" inquired Lord Vipe.

Ferr answered first, seeing as he was first in command when Vipe was away.

"Aww, you should've seen it. We were standing right here, guarding the scepter, and awaiting your return, when a little gnome showed up."

"Yeah," added Corv who put the gold away in his pocket. "He was kinda' creepy looking for a gnome. He wore way too much green if you ask me."

Vipe appeared impatient which was picked up by Ferr who continued the explanation, "Well, we tried to distract the little guy from knowing what we were doing, so we told him lots of frit jokes. You know, 'Knock, Knock, who's there? I forget.' Anyway, the little fella starts laughing like crazy, and gold falls from the sky. We just started picking it up when you came through."

Vipe took a piece of gold from Ferr, and watched as it slowly turned from gold to orange to brown. Then it turned from metal to a small cow pie. "What kind of sick joke is this?" he demanded.

Ferr and Corv shrugged their shoulders as Vipe shied the cow patties at them until they bowed with fear. Vipe wasted no more time getting to the point, "Well, where is the scepter now? I need it."

Ferr and Corv began frantically searching for the glorified baton.

"Umm, sir?" asked Corv who, being second in command, also had the duty of taking the blame for everything, "I think the gnome took it."

Vipe immediately swooshed his cape, turned to face the back wall of the trunk of the tree, and placed the key from his badge in the image of the key on the trunk. "When I get back, you better hope someone puts a spell on me to forget I ever knew you two!" With that, Vipe was whisked right back in front of Queen Oletta.

"Your majesty," he said as he bowed low and dusted his pants off at the same time.

"Do you have it? You do remember the plan, don't you?" The queen leaned in close, and waited for Vipe's answer, almost as if she knew what the answer would be.

"Your majesty, I believe that our agreement is off. I have discussed it among my colleagues, and have decided that we no longer require your services. We will find ElCa's birth car on our own."

Queen Oletta looked over by the forest path, and found a large boulder to sit upon. She adjusted her wings to avoid squashing them, and sat down. "You know, I thought you would do something like that, so I called for a little back-up, as he is known in my little pink book of contacts."

The queen, with swan-like grace, swept her arm to point with ballerina hands to a creature standing opposite them on the other side of the forest path. She pulled out some colorful bits from the small pocket at the waist of her tutu. She held them out in front of her and called, "Oh, Ian, look what I have for you."

Ian, the con, leprechaun leapt from his position on the other side of the trail to land perfectly on his toes on the queen's hand. He balanced himself with the scepter of power held perfectly perpendicular to his body.

The queen asked him, "Would you like to do a dance for me? I am offering refreshments."

All of the sudden, three leprechauns appeared on the forest path bearing a tiny fiddle, a badhran drum, and a small tin whistle. Ian directed them to begin playing an Irish ditty. Ian's toes began to tap as he danced a beautiful traditional Irish jig. It lasted only for a moment, leprechauns are so tiny, and their little hearts tucker out so quickly.

After his short performance, Ian dropped the scepter to grab some marshmallow shapes for nourishment and energy. The queen grabbed hold of her scepter as she lay Ian on the forest floor. Ian and his group of chieftains disappeared into the forest.

Vipe backed up to the Great Oak fumbling with his badge to get the key out.

The queen snapped her fingers, and Captain Jones, and six other gnomes, appeared and grabbed Vipe by the ankles to hold him still.

"Oh Lord Vipe, truly there can only be one royal in the forest, me. Now, about our plan. Yes, scrap it, dust it, forget it. That's what you frits are good at right?" The queen walked slowly towards Vipe pointing her scepter right at him.

The queen's scepter began to glow blue, and before Vipe could squeal his very last squeal, blue sparks emanated from its tips. Vipe was now twitching his nose. The queen had turned him into a mini rex rabbit.

The queen and the gnomes all had a good laugh; and she ordered the gnomes to search Vipe's cape pockets and such. Captain Jones returned to the queen with Vipe's Key-per badge and an old car key.

"Oh yes," she added looking at the bunny who was too scared to run. "I have been fascinated with the frit naming system for quite some time now. Truly, it's the only reason I watch your silly news in the first place. I had Lance search out some human car names that might contain the letters E-L-C-A. Of course, I am referring to ElCa's birth car. We believe it is an El Camino. If your little hippity hoppity legs have time to go searching the neighborhood for one, you may still be able to become the head, or should I say, the *ears* of the fritmunity." She looked behind her to make sure that the gnome troops were laughing at her joke.

The queen grabbed the rabbit by the extra fur on its neck. She placed it in her lap, and she tied ElCa's birth key around its neck with a leather string. Oletta could hardly contain her giggles as she explained to Vipe the predicament in which he found himself.

"Here is ElCa's birth key. Should you be able to gnaw through the car door with your ever so cute bunny teeth, you may be able to hop in. And should you be able to manipulate those furry little paws of yours, you just might be able to put his birth key in the ignition, though I highly doubt it. Now, off you go."

The queen took the tree key from off the back of Vipe's Key-per badge, and placed it into the shape of the key in the Great Oak. She grabbed Vipe's rabbit foot before the dust swirled around him and carried him through the tree. "Look how generous I am being. I have given you a rabbit's foot for luck. Bye-bye."

Vipe, as a rabbit, thumped to the floor of the Great Oak. He was now back in the human world, and could clearly see that Ferr and Corv were now sleeping on the job. He couldn't speak, as rabbits don't make much noise unless they are in pain. He couldn't slobber all over their faces as rabbits aren't naturally inclined to do so, but he could bite.

Vipe hopped over to Corv, and climbed up his chest. He chose carefully to bite a place which would definitely wake the sleeping frit.

Corv awoke to being bit squarely on the cheek by a tiny white rabbit with a key tied around its neck. He pushed the rabbit off of him, and kicked his friend Ferr until he awoke. "Rabies!" he yelled, and pointed to the ground.

Ferr saw that he was pointing at a tiny white rabbit.

"Rabies!" Corv cried again, and grabbed Ferr's vest. "Run like your dust depended on it. That rabid rabbit just bit me on the cheek. Now, I've got rabies!"

Ferr and Corv, as they slithered through the park, put on their security socks as there was just enough sunlight left to be seen.

20

Key-ping it real

Yo had traveled to school with Junior to go back to the Lost and Found Box. Everything he had found there the first time around had been taken from him, or fell out of his satchel when he fell on the queen at Barbahee. So he had returned to see what other treasures he could find; but to his disappointment, he found that the box had been emptied.

Yo was miserable. He didn't even wait to jump back into Junior's backpack to catch the bus back home. He left the school before the Ledge of Grievance was even said.

It had taken him nearly all day just to get to his next favorite place to be: the playground. He had just barely stepped into the meadow, and taken his sock off, when he was bowled over by two Key-pers.

"Run, I tell you," yelled Ferr.

"Like the wind, I say!" screamed Corv.

Yo was so used to being yelled at and falling down, that in his state of misery, he just stayed on the ground. He wondered why, this time, he was being run over and yelled at by complete strangers.

His thoughts were soon interrupted by the appearance of a cute white bunny which, incidentally, hopped right into his lap. "Oh how perfectly fritastic," Yo exclaimed as he gently lifted the tiny bunny to his chest.

"What's your name little fella'?" Yo waited as if the rabbit could speak, but it didn't.

Lord Vipe, now bunny, simply wondered if Yo would carry him around to look for an El Camino to try ElCa's key in. He knew if he acted cute enough that Yo just might take the bait; which he did.

Yo waited for a name that did not come, so he took it upon himself to name the rabbit. "I shall call you Goober II. Oh, wait!" Yo studied his bunny and found a key around its neck.

"Aww, it's like you were meant to be found by a frit. Is this your birth key?" Yo looked at the key which had the letters M-I-N-O on it, though they were worn and hard to read.

Yo said, "I guess I'll have to name you MINO!"

Again the rabbit said nothing. Yo put Mino/Lord Vipe in his backpack, which he was still wearing around the front, and began the one block walk over to Farmer Clark's yard right next door to the Fritscovery Newsroom.

"I think you look hungry, Mino. I know a perfect garden where you can eat," Yo said as he closed the flap of his backpack and started walking.

Amry and Onda had called ElCa on the birdie phone back at the station. "ElCa, sir, we need you to give one of your impressive speeches. Things have got to change. Yes, meet us at the auto graveyard behind

Mr. Paul's house. Yes, just two houses away from the Fritscovery Newsroom. Yes, use your key, you know, the dust swirly thing. We gotta do this now to have it ready for the 7:59."

The two best friends loaded up the camera gear and a new microphone, that Amry "borrowed" from Rove's anchorman desk. "He won't miss it, right?" said Amry as he rolled it up, and put it in his satchel. They both covered themselves with their socks, and waited by the edge of the VCR in the entertainment center.

Mr., Mrs., and Junior were watching the six o'clock news which was winding down. The two frits quickly jumped from the VCR to the entertainment center ledge, to the book shelf, to behind the couch. The quickly slid along the couch and the wall to the front door that Ishi was holding open, ever so cracked, so as not to draw Mrs. attention.

"Hey youfers," Ishi said, as Onda and Amry both held their forefingers to their lips.

"Ssh!" sounded Amry. "The family is in the living room. Make sure that Niss has the door open around 7:45. We're going to be cutting it close tonight."

Ishi was curious, "What is it this time? Did you catch a gnome?"

Amry and Onda shook their heads, and waved goodbye as they headed out the cracked open front door, over the driveway, turning left to go to the backyard. They had to hide behind a tree for a moment as Amry said, "Oh boy, Farmer Clark is in his barn getting the hose out to water the popsicles. We need to be careful not to be seen."

Amry pointed to the man pulling a dark green hose off of a roll by the barn, and sliding it down the hill to his garden.

The frits girded up their loins and made a mad dash behind the garden fence to the side yard of Mr. Paul, and eventually through a crack in the chain link fence of Mr. Paul's auto graveyard where they had first interviewed Odge or Vipe or Mino– whatever you want to call him at this point.

ElCa was there waiting for them on the same leather car bench that Odge had been standing behind.

Onda and Amry were glad to see him, and started to brief him immediately on the plan, "We're going to expose Lord Vipe as Odge. We're going to show the fritmunity that right here, in this very spot, Odge denounced his own organization." Amry pounded his fist where ElCa sat.

"Yes," said Onda. "And we're starting a new Key-per organization."

"Oh no," said ElCa. "That doesn't sound right."

Amry butted in, "ElCa, you'll see. We are forming the *Peace* Key-pers. We'll hold frits' birth keys, and keep them safe from the real Key-pers' clutches, to keep the peace. And we already have our first set of keys." Amry held up and jingled Odge's keys that were found in the garage.

ElCa smiled, "I am glad to see that you found those."

"What," said Amry looking confused. "What are you talking about?"

ElCa explained, "Before you came to see me about taking the scepter, I followed Lord Vipe to the garage where your birth car is located. As he placed your birth keys in your birth car's ignition; he had to lay down his keys that he was holding. I simply made him forget to pick them up."

Onda started to chastise the leader, "Hey, I thought frits couldn't make other frits forget. Isn't that against the rules?"

ElCa understood Onda's inquisition, "Well, it is actually *impossible* unless you're holding this. ElCa held up an interesting looking key from his belt. He removed it from the metal ring to which it was attached by a leather strap.

"Hey, that's your master key, right?" Amry held out his hand in the hopes that ElCa would let him hold it and look it over.

ElCa placed the Master key in Amry's hands and said, "This is more than the Master Key. It's the right to lead the tribe, and it's the key to something the fritmunity has lost. It's the key to our imagination. You simply hold the key up to your lips and speak what you imagine, and then you'll be there."

"Do you want to know why the frits can't enter the Magic Forest? Because they can't imagine it anymore, but *you* can Amry. Yes, you can!"

At that moment they all heard Yo yell, "Hey youfers, I got a new pet!" Yo was calling from the back of Farmer Clark's garden.

Amry, Onda, and ElCa all held up the *ssh* sign and pointed to Farmer Clark who was detangling the knots in the water hose.

Yo yelled back despite his friends warnings, "Don't worry, I made him forget what he was going to water." Yo took the white rabbit to Farmer Clark's garden gate, opened it, and let the rabbit jump it.

Onda turned to Amry and said, "I'll go get him before he is seen and caught. You know how well he spell speaks."

Onda put his sock on, ran through Mr. Paul's chain link fence to Farmer Clark's garden, and grabbed Yo by his backpack to drag him over to the auto graveyard.

Yo cried, "But what about my white rabbit?"

Onda answered, "You put him in the garden right? He can't get out. Don't worry about it. You can't take care of a rabbit anyway.

Just leave him there, before *you* get caught, and become somebody's pet."

Yo hung his head again murmuring, "But he had a key, and he was meant for me."

No one, but ElCa, heard Yo's mumbling. Amry and Onda were all too busy setting up for ElCa's big speech.

ElCa was looking earnestly across the graveyard to get a look at the rabbit with a key. "You said this rabbit had a key, eh?" ElCa sat down next to Yo, who had plopped down on the grass in desperation.

"Yes, it had the letters, M-I-N-O on it. I've always liked the letter 'M' so I knew the bunny was meant to be my pet."

"I see," said ElCa, who looked out across the yard, and saw that Farmer Clark had indeed *not* forgotten what to water. He was heading towards the garden, all the while stretching out and unwinding the garden hose.

ElCa knew, more than anyone else, that truly his seven years were up. He put his head in his hands and said, "It's time."

Just as Amry and Onda yelled towards him, "It's time ElCa, let's do this!"

Amry was sitting on the aqua bench right where Odge/Vipe/Mino had sat before. He waited until ElCa came over and sat down next to him before he motioned to Onda to roll the tape.

"Onda, put the old Odge interview in, run it all the way to the end, and then start recording me and ElCa."

Onda laughed as he gave the thumbs up sign; remembering all the trouble that one gesture had caused. He had already fast forwarded the tape and was ready to go.

Amry positioned his microphone and began the epilogue to the Key-per interview. "As you can see, or don't see, this defector – and we have this on good authority – is none other than the Key-per leader, Lord Vipe. He disguised himself as Odge, his real name, just to leave his own organization. You may be asking yourself, why I am revealing the identity of a Key-per in trouble. This is simple; because I have his birth key."

Amry held up the *Dodge Viper* keys in front of the camera and jingled them.

Amry continued, "No. I'm not becoming a Key-per. I'm bringing forth a new opportunity, a new solution to the fritmunity: the Peace Key-pers. No longer will we let some other group hold our life in their hands. Find your birth keys. Hold your own life in your own hands, and use that life for good."

"I say to Odge, come out of hiding. No one can hurt you now. Finders Keepers, Losers Weepers." Amry knew that Lord Vipe would be seething that his identity had been revealed in this awful manner. Lord Vipe's muscle, Ferr and Corv, and even his friend Tang, would be confused by Odge's cry for help so they might leave the organization.

Amry turned to ElCa, who was watching Farmer Clark enter his garden. Amry had to tap on the microphone to get his attention. "ElCa, sir, as the frit tribal leader, would you like to add words of encouragement to those threatened by Key-pers or otherwise saddened by the nomadic state of the frit?"

ElCa turned to the camera, held the microphone, and said, "To the fritmunity, I say…" ElCa was cut short by Farmer Clark yelling in his garden.

All the frits put on their socks, and crawled under the car bench as they heard Farmer Clark yell out, "A rabbit?! Get out of my garden, shoo, shoo!"

Then there was a small moment of silence until the yelling resumed, "What in the world? This can't be. Where did you get this? Who tied it around your neck?" Farmer Clark had caught the stunned bunny, and ran with it over to Mr. Paul's garage.

Amry turned to Yo, and asked, "What did you do now?"

"Nothing," said Yo, "This bunny just walked over to me, and wanted to be my pet. I just brought him to the garden to eat some fresh vegetables to keep his bunny fur nice and shiny."

All the frits listened for what might happen next. Mr. Paul opened the garage door and asked Farmer Clark what the matter was. Farmer Clark replied, "Do you remember that El Camino that I sold to you because I lost the key, and it cost too much to put in a new ignition?"

"Yes," said Mr. Paul, now very curious as why Farmer Clark was carrying a bunny with a key around its neck.

"Do you see this?" said Farmer Clark holding up the key tied around the bunny's neck.

"Yes, but I don't understand why a bunny would have it." Mr. Paul took the bunny, and looked it over. "Well, let's go see if it fits. I still have the car in the back junk yard."

As soon as ElCa heard this, he turned to Onda and said, "Turn the camera on, and point it at me. Amry, give me the microphone. Onda, make sure that Amry is in the camera's shot as well.'

Onda and Amry both did as they were told, and ElCa began talking quickly. "I have been your leader for just over seven years. Every year, I have pleaded our case to the AMCS. Our status has never been renewed, and maybe it's time for a new leader. I want this on film so that it can't be disputed. Amry, I entrust the Master key to you. You know its power, and you love the frits more than any frit I know. Tomorrow is voting day in the Magic Forest, and I know that you will represent the frit well."

Amry, stunned, took the belt that ElCa handed him, placed the key on it, and placed it around his waist.

ElCa took off his long over-robe, placed it over Amry's shoulders, and said, "And I support your idea of the Peace Key-pers. I hope this works out."

ElCa turned just in time to see Farmer Clark take the key off of the bunny and start his old El Camino. At which point, Amry, Onda, and Yo all witnessed the disappearance of ElCa, who left behind a string of dust.

Amry asked his friend, "Did you get all of that?"

"Yes, Master," said Onda who hugged both of his friends as they waited for Farmer Clark to drive the old El Camino off of the auto graveyard.

As soon as the car had passed out of a gate through the back, the three friends saw that the sun was going down.

Amry pulled out his watch from his satchel, "Uh, it's 7:30, youfers – RUN!" Then Amry stopped dead in his tracks, "Nope, no more running youfers. We're not running anymore." Amry held up the Master Key to his lips and said, "Imagine us right by the front door of the house which holds the Fritscovery Newsroom."

A dust swirl came down from above, scooped them up, and carried them to the front door of Junior's house. Niss was waiting for them, "Where's ElCa," he asked, noticing that only the three friends emerged from the dust cloud.

"Just watch the 7:59," said Yo, as they all passed through the front door of the house.

They slid between the couch and the wall of the living room, and made it to Saab in broadcasting, who said, "Rove is looking for his microphone. You'd better give it back."

Yo took the microphone from Amry. "I'll do it," he said, and ran towards the anchor desk.

Onda told Saab not to worry about the film going to editing, it's ready as is, just run it at 7:59.

When Yo entered the newsroom at 7:58, no one was there. Rove was looking for a replacement microphone, and Rove's cameraman, T-Bac, was looking for Rove. Yo knew he could save the day. Someone had to set everything up for when Saab ran the report in one minute.

Yo had hung around the newsroom, and Amry, practically his whole young adult life. He knew exactly what to do.

21

Yo, what's up?

Amry and Onda ran back to the Wind Star Style Salon to remind the girls to watch the news, but they needed no reminder. The fritmunity had all heard about the gnomes and such, and were dying to see what it was all about. And boy did they get more than what they bargained for. Amry saw that everyone had left the salon to watch the TV in the living room that had been left on. Olet had already changed the channel to the Public Access Channel. Amry looked at his watch to see that it was exactly 7:59.

They all stood in amazement, especially Olet, as they watched her brother, Yo, fill in for Rove.

"Yo here for what's up in the frit world. Tonight a stunning event occurred. Only Amry, our local reporter, has it caught on tape."

Amry's interview with Odge ran smoothly which segued into ElCa passing the Master key to Amry and disappearing.

After the report ended, Yo added, *"Congratulations to our new leader, a dear friend of mine who is compassionate, loyal, and caring. May he do well at the vote tomorrow. We wish him all the luck, non-leprechaun luck that is."*

Star led the group back to the salon, and gawked at Amry, who was fiddling with the belt, and the robe, to make it fit.

He didn't know what to say, and before he could think to say anything, three Key-pers entered through the dryer sheet door of the salon.

It was Ferr, Corv, and Tang, who was looking more disheveled than ever. Ferr grabbed Amry by the shoulders and shook him, "Where's our leader?"

"Yeah," added Corv. "What did you do with him?"

"Yeah Amry, who's the bad guy now? *I* never took anyone's birth keys," said Tang.

Ferr let go of Amry, but started overturning the laundry lid chairs, "If you don't tell us; I'll trash this place."

"Better yet," said Corv, "How about we trash you?"

Wind and Star stood in between the Key-pers and Amry, and said, "Amry, Don't you have a meeting to go to tomorrow? I suggest you get ready."

"But what about your salon?" he asked.

Star said, "Oh, don't worry. These two have been in need of a hair cut for years." Star pulled out her scissors, and held them in front of her like a sword.

Amry waved goodbye to his friends, blew a kiss to Olet, and whispered into the key.

The dust was so thick swirling around Amry that the Key-pers left to avoid choking, while the rest of the salon hid under laundry detergent lids to avoid it as well.

The morning report at 7:59 a.m. went a little something like this: *"Yo here, for 'what's up'. I will be your morning news anchor. And starting off this morning we have a tragic story. One frit has gone missing: the frit in the interview last night, Odge, otherwise known as Lord Vipe. He was last seen in the playground meadow by his Key-per friends Ferr and Corv. Should you have any information of his whereabouts, please call the station.*

In other news today, the Ancient Magical Creature Status of the frit is to be voted on at noon. We will have the full report tonight at 7:59."

Printed in the United States
69970LV00011B/25-39

9 781425 923396